# Charles Dickens – Our Bore & Other Short Stories

Charles Dickens (1812-1870) is regarded by many readers and literary critics to be THE major English novelist of the Victorian Age. He is remembered today as the author of a series of weighty novels which have been translated into many languages and promoted to the rank of World Classics. The latter include, but are not limited to, *The Adventures of Oliver Twist*, *A Tale of Two Cities*, *David Copperfield*, *A Christmas Carol*, *Hard Times*, *Great Expectations* and *The Old Curiosity Shop*.

Here we bring you a selection of his quite remarkable short stories.

## Contents

## Our School

We went to look at it, only this last Midsummer, and found that the Railway had cut up root and branch. A great trunk-line had swallowed the playground, sliced away the schoolroom, and pared off the corner of the house: which, thus curtailed of its proportions, presented itself, in a green stage of stucco, profilewise towards the road, like a forlorn flat-iron without a handle, standing on end.

It seems as if our schools were doomed to be the sport of change. We have faint recollections of a Preparatory Day-School, which we have sought in vain, and which must have been pulled down to make a new street, ages ago. We have dim impressions, scarcely amounting to a belief, that it was over a dyer's shop. We know that you went up steps to it; that you frequently grazed your knees in doing so; that you generally got your leg over the scraper, in trying to scrape the mud off a very unsteady little shoe. The mistress of the Establishment holds no place in our memory; but, rampant on one eternal door-mat, in an eternal entry long and narrow, is a puffy pug-dog, with a personal animosity towards us, who triumphs over Time. The bark of that baleful Pug, a certain radiating way he had of snapping at our undefended legs, the ghastly grinning of his moist black muzzle and white teeth, and the insolence of his crisp tail curled like a pastoral crook, all live and flourish. From an otherwise unaccountable association of him with a fiddle, we conclude that he was of French extraction, and his name FIDELE. He belonged to some female, chiefly inhabiting a back-parlour, whose life appears to us to have been consumed in sniffing, and in wearing a brown beaver bonnet. For her, he would sit up and balance cake upon his nose, and not eat it until twenty had been counted. To the best of our belief we were once called in to witness this performance; when, unable, even in his milder moments, to endure our presence, he instantly made at us, cake and all.

Why a something in mourning, called 'Miss Frost,' should still connect itself with our preparatory school, we are unable to say. We retain no impression of the beauty of Miss Frost - if she were beautiful; or of the mental fascinations of Miss Frost - if she were accomplished; yet her name and her black dress hold an enduring place in our remembrance. An equally impersonal boy, whose name has long since shaped itself unalterably into 'Master Mawls,' is not to be dislodged from our brain. Retaining no vindictive feeling towards Mawls - no feeling whatever, indeed - we infer that neither he nor we can have loved Miss Frost. Our first impression of Death and Burial is associated with this formless pair. We all three nestled awfully in a corner one wintry day, when the wind was blowing shrill, with Miss Frost's pinafore over our heads; and Miss Frost told us in a whisper about somebody being 'screwed down.' It is the only distinct recollection we preserve of these impalpable creatures, except a suspicion that the manners of Master Mawls were susceptible of much improvement. Generally speaking, we may observe that whenever we see a child intently occupied with its nose, to the exclusion of all other subjects of interest, our mind reverts, in a flash, to Master Mawls.

But, the School that was Our School before the Railroad came and overthrew it, was quite another sort of place. We were old enough to be put into Virgil when we went there, and to get Prizes for a variety of polishing on which the rust has long accumulated. It was a School of some celebrity in its neighbourhood - nobody could have said why - and we had the honour to attain and hold the eminent position of first boy. The master was supposed among us to know nothing, and one of the ushers was supposed to know everything. We are still inclined to think the first-named supposition perfectly correct.

We have a general idea that its subject had been in the leather trade, and had bought us - meaning Our School - of another proprietor who was immensely learned. Whether this belief had any real foundation, we are not likely ever to know now. The only branches of education with which he showed the least acquaintance, were, ruling and corporally punishing. He was always ruling ciphering-books with a bloated mahogany ruler, or smiting the palms of offenders with the same diabolical instrument, or viciously drawing a pair of pantaloons tight with one of his large hands, and caning the wearer with the other. We have no doubt whatever that this occupation was the principal solace of his existence.

A profound respect for money pervaded Our School, which was, of course, derived from its Chief. We remember an idiotic goggle-eyed boy, with a big head and half-crowns without end, who suddenly appeared as a parlour-boarder, and was rumoured to have come by sea from some mysterious part of the earth where his parents rolled in gold. He was usually called 'Mr.' by the Chief, and was said to feed in the parlour on steaks and gravy; likewise to drink currant wine. And he openly stated that if rolls and coffee were ever denied him at breakfast, he would write home to that unknown part of the globe from which he had come, and cause himself to be recalled to the regions of gold. He was put into no form or class, but learnt alone, as little as he liked - and he liked very little - and there was a belief among that this was because he was too wealthy to be 'taken down.' His special treatment, and our vague association of him with the sea, and with storms, and sharks, and Coral Reefs occasioned the wildest legends to be circulated as his history. A tragedy in blank verse was written on the subject - if our memory does not deceive us, by the hand that now chronicles these recollections - in which his father figured as a Pirate, and was shot for a voluminous catalogue of atrocities: first imparting to his wife the secret of the cave in which his wealth was stored, and from which his only son's half-crowns now issued. Dumbledon (the boy's name) was represented as 'yet unborn' when his brave father met his fate; and the despair and grief of Mrs. Dumbledon at that calamity was movingly shadowed forth as having weakened the parlour-boarder's mind. This production was received with great favour, and was twice performed with closed doors in the dining- room. But, it got wind, and was seized as libellous, and brought the unlucky poet into severe affliction. Some two years afterwards, all of a sudden one day, Dumbledon vanished. It was whispered that the Chief himself had taken him down to the Docks, and re-shipped him for the Spanish Main; but nothing certain was ever known about his disappearance. At this hour, we cannot thoroughly disconnect him from California.

Our School was rather famous for mysterious pupils. There was another - a heavy young man, with a large double-cased silver watch, and a fat knife the handle of which was a perfect tool-box - who unaccountably appeared one day at a special desk of his own, erected close to that of the Chief, with whom he held familiar converse. He lived in the parlour, and went out for his walks, and never took the least notice of us - even of us, the first boy - unless to give us a deprecatory kick, or grimly to take our hat off and throw it away, when he encountered us out of doors, which unpleasant ceremony he always performed as he passed - not even condescending to stop for the purpose. Some of us believed that the classical attainments of this phenomenon were terrific, but that his penmanship and arithmetic were defective, and he had come there to mend them; others, that he was going to set up a school, and had paid the Chief 'twenty-five pound down,' for leave to see Our School at work. The gloomier spirits even said that he was going to buy us; against which contingency, conspiracies were set on foot for a general defection and running away. However, he never did that. After staying for a quarter, during which period, though closely observed, he was never seen to do anything but make pens out of quills, write small hand in a secret portfolio, and punch the point of the sharpest blade in his knife into his desk all over it, he too disappeared, and his place knew him no more.

There was another boy, a fair, meek boy, with a delicate complexion and rich curling hair, who, we found out, or thought we found out (we have no idea now, and probably had none then, on what grounds, but it was confidentially revealed from mouth to mouth), was the son of a Viscount who had deserted his lovely mother. It was understood that if he had his rights, he would be worth twenty thousand a year. And that if his mother ever met his father, she would shoot him with a silver pistol, which she carried, always loaded to the muzzle, for that purpose. He was a very suggestive topic. So was a young Mulatto, who was always believed (though very amiable) to have a dagger about him somewhere. But, we think they were both outshone, upon the whole, by another boy who claimed to have been born on the twenty-ninth of February, and to have only one birthday in five years. We suspect this to have been a fiction - but he lived upon it all the time he was at Our School.

The principal currency of Our School was slate pencil. It had some inexplicable value, that was never ascertained, never reduced to a standard. To have a great hoard of it was somehow to be rich. We used to bestow it in charity, and confer it as a precious boon upon our chosen friends. When the holidays were coming, contributions were solicited for certain boys whose relatives were in India, and who were appealed for under the generic name of 'Holiday-stoppers,' - appropriate marks of remembrance that should enliven and cheer them in their homeless state. Personally, we always contributed these tokens of sympathy in the form of slate pencil, and always felt that it would be a comfort and a treasure to them.

Our School was remarkable for white mice. Red-polls, linnets, and even canaries, were kept in desks, drawers, hat-boxes, and other strange refuges for birds; but white mice were the favourite stock. The boys trained the mice, much better than the masters trained the boys. We recall one white mouse, who lived in the cover of a Latin dictionary, who ran up ladders, drew Roman chariots, shouldered muskets, turned wheels, and even made a very creditable appearance on the stage as the Dog of Montargis. He might have achieved greater things, but for having the misfortune to mistake his way in a triumphal procession to the Capitol, when he fell into a deep inkstand, and was dyed black and drowned. The mice were the occasion of some most ingenious engineering, in the construction of their houses and instruments of performance. The famous one belonged to a company of proprietors, some of whom have since made Railroads, Engines, and Telegraphs; the chairman has erected mills and bridges in New Zealand.

The usher at Our School, who was considered to know everything as opposed to the Chief, who was considered to know nothing, was a bony, gentle-faced, clerical-looking young man in rusty black. It was whispered that he was sweet upon one of Maxby's sisters (Maxby lived close by, and was a day pupil), and further that he 'favoured Maxby.' As we remember, he taught Italian to Maxby's sisters on half-holidays. He once went to the play with them, and wore a white waistcoat and a rose: which was considered among us equivalent to a declaration. We were of opinion on that occasion, that to the last moment he expected Maxby's father to ask him to dinner at five o'clock, and therefore neglected his own dinner at half-past one, and finally got none. We exaggerated in our imaginations the extent to which he punished Maxby's father's cold meat at supper; and we agreed to believe that he was elevated with wine and water when he came home. But, we all liked him; for he had a good knowledge of boys, and would have made it a much better school if he had had more power. He was writing master, mathematical master, English master made out the bills, mended the pens, and did all sorts of things. He divided the little boys with the Latin master (they were smuggled through their rudimentary books, at odd times when there was nothing else to do), and he always called at parents' houses to inquire after sick boys, because he had gentlemanly manners. He was rather musical, and on some remote quarter-day had bought an old trombone; but bit of it was lost, and it made the most extraordinary sounds when he sometimes tried to play it of an evening. His holidays never began (on account of the bills) until long after ours; but, in the summer vacations he used to take pedestrian excursions with a knapsack; and at Christmas time, he went to see his father at Chipping Norton, who we all said (on no authority) was a dairy-fed pork- butcher. Poor fellow! He was very low all day on Maxby's sister's wedding-day, and afterwards was thought to favour Maxby more than ever, though he had been expected to spite him. He has been dead these twenty years. Poor fellow!

Our remembrance of Our School, presents the Latin master as a colourless doubled-up near-sighted man with a crutch, who was always cold, and always putting onions into his ears for deafness, and always disclosing ends of flannel under all his garments, and almost always applying a ball of pocket-handkerchief to some part of his face with a screwing action round and round. He was a very good scholar, and took great pains where he saw intelligence and a desire to learn: otherwise, perhaps not. Our memory presents him (unless teased into a passion) with as little energy as colour - as having been worried and tormented into monotonous feebleness - as having had the best part of his life ground out of him in a Mill of boys. We remember with terror how he fell asleep one sultry afternoon with the little smuggled class before him, and awoke not when the footstep of the Chief fell heavy on the floor; how the Chief aroused him, in the midst of a dread silence, and said, 'Mr. Blinkins, are you ill, sir?' how he blushingly replied, 'Sir, rather so;' how the Chief retorted with severity, 'Mr. Blinkins, this is no place to be ill in' (which was very, very true), and walked back solemn as the ghost in Hamlet, until, catching a wandering eye, he called that boy for inattention, and happily expressed his feelings towards the Latin master through the medium of a substitute.

There was a fat little dancing-master who used to come in a gig, and taught the more advanced among us hornpipes (as an accomplishment in great social demand in after life); and there was a brisk little French master who used to come in the sunniest weather, with a handleless umbrella, and to whom the Chief was always polite, because (as we believed), if the Chief offended him, he would instantly address the Chief in French, and for ever confound him before the boys with his inability to understand or reply.

There was besides, a serving man, whose name was Phil. Our retrospective glance presents Phil as a shipwrecked carpenter, cast away upon the desert island of a school, and carrying into practice an ingenious inkling of many trades. He mended whatever was broken, and made whatever was wanted. He was general glazier, among other things, and mended all the broken windows - at the prime cost (as was darkly rumoured among us) of ninepence, for every square charged three-and-six to parents. We had a high opinion of his mechanical genius, and generally held that the Chief 'knew something bad of him,' and on pain of divulgence enforced Phil to be his bondsman. We particularly remember that Phil had a sovereign contempt for learning: which engenders in us a respect for his sagacity, as it implies his accurate observation of the relative positions of the Chief and the ushers. He was an impenetrable man, who waited at table between whiles, and throughout 'the half' kept the boxes in severe custody. He was morose, even to the Chief, and never smiled, except at breaking-up, when, in acknowledgment of the toast, 'Success to Phil! Hooray!' he would slowly carve a grin out of his wooden face, where it would remain until we were all gone. Nevertheless, one time when we had the scarlet fever in the school, Phil nursed all the sick boys of his own accord, and was like a mother to them.

There was another school not far off, and of course Our School could have nothing to say to that school. It is mostly the way with schools, whether of boys or men. Well! the railway has swallowed up ours, and the locomotives now run smoothly over its ashes.

So fades and languishes, grows dim and dies,
All that this world is proud of,

- and is not proud of, too. It had little reason to be proud of Our School, and has done much better since in that way, and will do far better yet.

# The Dancing Academy

Of all the dancing academies that ever were established, there never was one more popular in its immediate vicinity than Signor Billsmethi's, of the 'King's Theatre.' It was not in Spring- gardens, or Newman-street, or Berners-street, or Gower-street, or Charlotte-street, or Percy-street, or any other of the numerous streets which have been devoted time out of mind to professional people, dispensaries, and boarding-houses; it was not in the West-end at all, it rather approximated to the eastern portion of London, being situated in the populous and improving neighbourhood of Gray's-inn-lane. It was not a dear dancing academy, four-and-sixpence a quarter is decidedly cheap upon the whole. It was VERY select, the number of pupils being strictly limited to seventy- five, and a quarter's payment in advance being rigidly exacted. There was public tuition and private tuition, an assembly-room and a parlour. Signor Billsmethi's family were always thrown in with the parlour, and included in parlour price; that is to say, a private pupil had Signor Billsmethi's parlour to dance IN, and Signor Billsmethi's family to dance WITH; and when he had been sufficiently broken in in the parlour, he began to run in couples in the assembly-room.

Such was the dancing academy of Signor Billsmethi, when Mr. Augustus Cooper, of Fetter-lane, first saw an unstamped advertisement walking leisurely down Holborn-hill, announcing to the world that Signor Billsmethi, of the King's Theatre, intended opening for the season with a Grand Ball.

Now, Mr. Augustus Cooper was in the oil and colour line, just of age, with a little money, a little business, and a little mother, who, having managed her husband and HIS business in his lifetime, took to managing her son and HIS business after his decease; and so, somehow or other, he had been cooped up in the little back parlour behind the shop on week-days, and in a little deal box without a lid (called by courtesy a pew) at Bethel Chapel, on Sundays, and had seen no more of the world than if he had been an infant all his days; whereas Young White, at the gas-fitter's over the way, three years younger than him, had been flaring away like winkin', going to the theatre, supping at harmonic meetings, eating oysters by the barrel, drinking stout by the gallon, even out all night, and coming home as cool in the morning as if nothing had happened. So Mr. Augustus Cooper made up his mind that he would not stand it any longer, and had that very morning expressed to his mother a firm determination to be 'blowed,' in the event of his not being instantly provided with a street-door key. And he was walking down Holborn-hill, thinking about all these things, and wondering how he could manage to get introduced into genteel society for the first time, when his eyes rested on Signor Billsmethi's announcement, which it immediately struck him was just the very thing he wanted, for he should not only be able to select a genteel circle of acquaintance at once, out of the five-and- seventy pupils at four-and-sixpence a quarter, but should qualify himself at the same time to go through a hornpipe in private society, with perfect ease to himself and great delight to his friends. So, he stopped the unstamped advertisement, an animated sandwich, composed of a boy between two boards, and having procured a very small card with the Signor's address indented thereon, walked straight at once to the Signor's house, and very fast he walked too, for fear the list should be filled up, and the five- and-seventy completed, before he got there. The Signor was at home, and, what was still more gratifying, he was an Englishman! Such a nice man, and so polite! The list was not full, but it was a most extraordinary circumstance that there was only just one vacancy, and even that one would have been filled up, that very morning, only Signor Billsmethi was dissatisfied with the reference, and, being very much afraid that the lady wasn't select, wouldn't take her.

'And very much delighted I am, Mr. Cooper,' said Signor Billsmethi, 'that I did NOT take her. I assure you, Mr. Cooper, I don't say it to flatter you, for I know you're above it, that I consider myself extremely fortunate in having a gentleman of your manners and appearance, sir.'

'I am very glad of it too, sir,' said Augustus Cooper.

'And I hope we shall be better acquainted, sir,' said Signor Billsmethi.

'And I'm sure I hope we shall too, sir,' responded Augustus Cooper. Just then, the door opened, and in came a young lady, with her hair curled in a crop all over her head, and her shoes tied in sandals all over her ankles.

'Don't run away, my dear,' said Signor Billsmethi; for the young lady didn't know Mr. Cooper was there when she ran in, and was going to run out again in her modesty, and in confusion-like. 'Don't run away, my dear,' said Signor Billsmethi, 'this is Mr. Cooper, Mr. Cooper, of Fetter-lane. Mr. Cooper, my daughter, sir, Miss Billsmethi, sir, who I hope will have the pleasure of dancing many a quadrille, minuet, gavotte, country-dance, fandango, double-hornpipe, and farinagholkajingo with you, sir. She dances them all, sir; and so shall you, sir, before you're a quarter older, sir.'

And Signor Bellsmethi slapped Mr. Augustus Cooper on the back, as if he had known him a dozen years, so friendly; and Mr. Cooper bowed to the young lady, and the young lady curtseyed to him, and Signor Billsmethi said they were as handsome a pair as ever he'd wish to see; upon which the young lady exclaimed, 'Lor, pa!' and blushed as red as Mr. Cooper himself, you might have thought they were both standing under a red lamp at a chemist's shop; and before Mr. Cooper went away it was settled that he should join the family circle that very night, taking them just as they were, no ceremony nor nonsense of that kind, and learn his positions in order that he might lose no time, and be able to come out at the forthcoming ball.

Well; Mr. Augustus Cooper went away to one of the cheap shoemakers' shops in Holborn, where gentlemen's dress-pumps are seven-and- sixpence, and men's strong walking just nothing at all, and bought a pair of the regular seven-and- sixpenny, long-quartered, town- mades, in which he astonished himself quite as much as his mother, and sallied forth to Signor Billsmethi's. There were four other private pupils in the parlour: two ladies and two gentlemen. Such nice people! Not a bit of pride about them. One of the ladies in particular, who was in training for a Columbine, was remarkably affable; and she and Miss Billsmethi took such an interest in Mr. Augustus Cooper, and joked, and smiled, and looked so bewitching, that he got quite at home, and learnt his steps in no time. After the practising was over, Signor Billsmethi, and Miss Billsmethi, and Master Billsmethi, and a young lady, and the two ladies, and the two gentlemen, danced a quadrille, none of your slipping and sliding about, but regular warm work, flying into corners, and diving among chairs, and shooting out at the door, something like dancing! Signor Billsmethi in particular, notwithstanding his having a little fiddle to play all the time, was out on the landing every figure, and Master Billsmethi, when everybody else was breathless, danced a hornpipe, with a cane in his hand, and a cheese-plate on his head, to the unqualified admiration of the whole company. Then, Signor Billsmethi insisted, as they were so happy, that they should all stay to supper, and proposed sending Master Billsmethi for the beer and spirits, whereupon the two gentlemen swore, 'strike 'em wulgar if they'd stand that;' and were just going to quarrel who should pay for it, when Mr. Augustus Cooper said he would, if they'd have the kindness to allow him and they HAD the kindness to allow him; and Master Billsmethi brought the beer in a can, and the rum in a quart pot. They had a regular night of it; and Miss Billsmethi squeezed Mr. Augustus Cooper's hand under the table; and Mr. Augustus Cooper returned the squeeze, and returned home too, at something to six o'clock in the morning, when he was put to bed by main force by the apprentice, after repeatedly expressing an uncontrollable desire to pitch his revered parent out of the second-floor window, and to throttle the apprentice with his own neck-handkerchief.

Weeks had worn on, and the seven-and-sixpenny town-mades had nearly worn out when the night arrived for the grand dress-ball at which the whole of the five-and-seventy pupils were to meet together, for the first time that season, and to take out some portion of their respective four-and-sixpences in lamp-oil and fiddlers. Mr. Augustus Cooper had ordered a new coat for the occasion, a two- pound-tenner from Turnstile. It was his first appearance in public; and, after a grand Sicilian shawl-dance by fourteen young ladies in character, he was to open the quadrille department with Miss Billsmethi herself, with whom he had become quite intimate since his first introduction. It WAS a night! Everything was admirably arranged. The sandwich-boy took the hats and bonnets at the street-door; there was a turn-up bedstead in the back parlour, on which Miss Billsmethi made tea and coffee for such of the gentlemen as chose to pay for it, and such of the ladies as the gentlemen treated; red port-wine negus and lemonade were handed round at eighteen-pence head; and in pursuance of a previous engagement with the public-house at the corner of the street, an extra potboy was laid on for the occasion. In short, nothing could exceed the arrangements, except the company. Such ladies! Such pink silk stockings! Such artificial flowers! Such a number of cabs! No sooner had one cab set down a couple of ladies, than another cab drove up and set down another couple of ladies, and they all knew: not only one another, but the majority of the gentlemen into the bargain, which made it all as pleasant and lively as could be. Signor Billsmethi, in black tights, with a large blue bow in his buttonhole, introduced the ladies to such of the gentlemen as were strangers: and the ladies talked away, and laughed they did, it was delightful to see them.

As to the shawl-dance, it was the most exciting thing that ever was beheld; there was such a whisking, and rustling, and fanning, and getting ladies into a tangle wit artificial flowers, and then disentangling them again! And as to Mr. Augustus Cooper's share in the quadrille, he got through it admirably. He was missing from his partner, now and then, certainly, and discovered on such occasions to be either dancing with laudable perseverance in another set, or sliding about in perspective, without any definite object; but, generally speaking, they managed to shove him through the figure, until he turned up in the right place. Be this as it may, when he had finished, a great many ladies and gentlemen came up and complimented him very much, and said they had never seen a beginner do anything like it before; and Mr. Augustus Cooper was perfectly satisfied with himself, and everybody else into the bargain; and 'stood' considerable quantities of spirits-and-water, negus, and compounds, for the use and behoof of two or three dozen very particular friends, selected from the select circle of five- and-seventy pupils.

Now, whether it was the strength of the compounds, or the beauty of the ladies, or what not, it did so happen that Mr. Augustus Cooper encouraged, rather than repelled, the very flattering attentions of a young lady in brown gauze over white calico who had appeared particularly struck with him from the first; and when the encouragements had been prolonged for some time, Miss Billsmethi betrayed her spite and jealousy thereat by calling the young lady in brown gauze a 'creeter,' which induced the young lady in brown gauze to retort, in certain sentences containing a taunt founded on the payment of four-and-sixpence a quarter, which reference Mr. Augustus Cooper, being then and there in a state of considerable bewilderment, expressed his entire concurrence in. Miss Billsmethi, thus renounced, forthwith began screaming in the loudest key of her voice, at the rate of fourteen screams a minute; and being unsuccessful, in an onslaught on the eyes and face, first of the lady in gauze and then of Mr. Augustus Cooper, called distractedly on the other three-and-seventy pupils to furnish her with oxalic acid for her own private drinking; and, the call not being honoured, made another rush at Mr. Cooper, and then had her stay-lace cut, and was carried off to bed. Mr. Augustus Cooper, not being remarkable for quickness of apprehension, was at a loss to understand what all this meant, until Signor Billsmethi explained it in a most satisfactory manner, by stating to the pupils, that Mr. Augustus Cooper had made and confirmed divers promises of marriage to his daughter on divers occasions, and had now basely deserted her; on which, the indignation of the pupils became universal; and as several chivalrous gentlemen inquired rather pressingly of Mr. Augustus Cooper, whether he required anything for his own use, or, in other words, whether he wanted anything for himself,' he deemed it prudent to make a precipitate retreat. And the upshot of the matter was, that a lawyer's letter came next day, and an action was commenced next week; and that Mr. Augustus Cooper, after walking twice to the Serpentine for the purpose of drowning himself, and coming twice back without doing it, made a confidante of his mother, who compromised the matter with twenty pounds from the till: which made twenty pounds four shillings and sixpence paid to Signor Billsmethi, exclusive of treats and pumps. And Mr. Augustus Cooper went back and lived with his mother, and there he lives to this day; and as he has lost his ambition for society, and never goes into the world, he will never see his account of himself, and will never be any the wiser.

# The Hospital Patient

In our rambles through the streets of London after evening has set in, we often pause beneath the windows of some public hospital, and picture to ourself the gloomy and mournful scenes that are passing within. The sudden moving of a taper as its feeble ray shoots from window to window, until its light gradually disappears, as if it were carried farther back into the room to the bedside of some suffering patient, is enough to awaken a whole crowd of reflections; the mere glimmering of the low-burning lamps, which, when all other habitations are wrapped in darkness and slumber, denote the chamber where so many forms are writhing with pain, or wasting with disease, is sufficient to check the most boisterous merriment.

Who can tell the anguish of those weary hours, when the only sound the sick man hears, is the disjointed wanderings of some feverish slumberer near him, the low moan of pain, or perhaps the muttered, long-forgotten prayer of a dying man? Who, but they who have felt it, can imagine the sense of loneliness and desolation which must be the portion of those who in the hour of dangerous illness are left to be tended by strangers; for what hands, be they ever so gentle, can wipe the clammy brow, or smooth the restless bed, like those of mother, wife, or child?

Impressed with these thoughts, we have turned away, through the nearly-deserted streets; and the sight of the few miserable creatures still hovering about them, has not tended to lessen the pain which such meditations awaken. The hospital is a refuge and resting-place for hundreds, who but for such institutions must die in the streets and doorways; but what can be the feelings of some outcasts when they are stretched on the bed of sickness with scarcely a hope of recovery? The wretched woman who lingers about the pavement, hours after midnight, and the miserable shadow of a man, the ghastly remnant that want and drunkenness have left, which crouches beneath a window-ledge, to sleep where there is some shelter from the rain, have little to bind them to life, but what have they to look back upon, in death What are the unwonted comforts of a roof and a bed, to them, when the recollections of a whole life of debasement stalk before them; when repentance seems a mockery, and sorrow comes too late?

About a twelvemonth ago, as we were strolling through Covent-garden (we had been thinking about these things over-night), we were attracted by the very prepossessing appearance of a pickpocket, who having declined to take the trouble of walking to the Police- office, on the ground that he hadn't the slightest wish to go there at all, was being conveyed thither in a wheelbarrow, to the huge delight of a crowd.

Somehow, we never can resist joining a crowd, so we turned back with the mob, and entered the office, in company with our friend the pickpocket, a couple of policemen, and as many dirty-faced spectators as could squeeze their way in.

There was a powerful, ill-looking young fellow at the bar, who was undergoing an examination, on the very common charge of having, on the previous night, ill-treated a woman, with whom he lived in some court hard by. Several witnesses bor testimony to acts of the grossest brutality; and a certificate was read from the house- surgeon of a neighbouring hospital, describing the nature of the injuries the woman had received, and intimating that her recovery was extremely doubtful.

Some question appeared to have been raised about the identity of the prisoner; for when it was agreed that the two magistrates should visit the hospital at eight o'clock that evening, to take her deposition, it was settled that the man should be taken there also. He turned pale at this, and we saw him clench the bar very hard when the order was given. He was removed directly afterwards, and he spoke not a word.

We felt an irrepressible curiosity to witness this interview, although it is hard to tell why, at this instant, for we knew it must be a painful one. It was no very difficult matter for us to gain permission, and we obtained it.

The prisoner, and the officer who had him in custody, were already at the hospital when we reached it, and waiting the arrival of the magistrates in a small room below stairs. The man was handcuffed, and his hat was pulled forward over his eyes. It was easy to see, though, by the whiteness of his countenance, and the constant twitching of the muscles of his face, that he dreaded what was to come. After a short interval, the magistrates and clerk were bowed in by the house-surgeon and a couple of young men who smelt very strong of tobacco-smoke, they were introduced as 'dressers' and after one magistrate had complained bitterly of the cold, and the other of the absence of any news in the evening paper, it was announced that the patient was prepared; and we were conducted to the 'casualty ward' in which she was lying.

The dim light which burnt in the spacious room, increased rather than diminished the ghastly appearance of the hapless creatures in the beds, which were ranged in two long rows on either side. In one bed, lay a child enveloped in bandages, with its body half-consumed by fire; in another, a female, rendered hideous by some dreadful accident, was wildly beating her clenched fists on the coverlet, in pain; on a third, there lay stretched a young girl, apparently in the heavy stupor often the immediate precursor of death: her face was stained with blood, and her breast and arms were bound up in folds of linen. Two or three of the beds were empty, and their recent occupants were sitting beside them, but with faces so wan, and eyes so bright and glassy, that it was fearful to meet their gaze. On every face was stamped the expression of anguish and suffering.

The object of the visit was lying at the upper end of the room. She was a fine young woman of about two or three and twenty. Her long black hair, which had been hastily cut from near the wounds on her head, streamed over the pillow in jagged and matted locks. Her face bore deep marks of the ill-usage she had received: her hand was pressed upon her side, as if her chief pain were there; her breathing was short and heavy; and it was plain to see that she was dying fast. She murmured a few words in reply to the magistrate's inquiry whether she was in great pain; and, having been raised on the pillow by the nurse, looked vacantly upon the strange countenances that surrounded her bed. The magistrate nodded to the officer, to bring the man forward. He did so, and stationed him at the bedside. The girl looked on with a wild and troubled expression of face; but her sight was dim, and she did not know him.

'Take off his hat,' said the magistrate. The officer did as he was desired, and the man's features were disclosed.

The girl started up, with an energy quite preternatural; the fire gleamed in her heavy eyes, and the blood rushed to her pale and sunken cheeks. It was a convulsive effort. She fell back upon her pillow, and covering her scarred and bruised face with her hands, burst into tears. The man cast an anxious look towards her, but otherwise appeared wholly unmoved. After a brief pause the nature of the errand was explained, and the oath tendered.

'Oh, no, gentlemen,' said the girl, raising herself once more, and folding her hands together; 'no, gentlemen, for God's sake! I did it myself, it was nobody's fault, it was an accident. He didn't hurt me; he wouldn't for all the world. Jack, dear Jack, you know you wouldn't!'

Her sight was fast failing her, and her hand groped over the bedclothes in search of his. Brute as the man was, he was not prepared for this. He turned his face from the bed, and sobbed. The girl's colour changed, and her breathing grew more difficult. She was evidently dying.

'We respect the feelings which prompt you to this,' said the gentleman who had spoken first, 'but let me warn you, not to persist in what you know to be untrue, until it is too late. It cannot save him.'

'Jack,' murmured the girl, laying her hand upon his arm, 'they shall not persuade me to swear your life away. He didn't do it, gentlemen. He never hurt me.' She grasped his arm tightly, and added, in a broken whisper, 'I hope God Almighty will forgive me all the wrong I have done, and the life I have led. God bless you, Jack. Some kind gentleman take my love to my poor old father. Five years ago, he said he wished I had died a child. Oh, I wish I had! I wish I had!'

The nurse bent over the girl for a few seconds, and then drew the sheet over her face. It covered a corpse.

# The Boarding-House

### CHAPTER I.

Mrs. Tibbs was, beyond all dispute, the most tidy, fidgety, thrifty little personage that ever inhaled the smoke of London; and the house of Mrs. Tibbs was, decidedly, the neatest in all Great Coram- street. The area and the area-steps, and the street-door and the street-door steps, and the brass handle, and the door-plate, and the knocker, and the fan-light, were all as clean and bright, as indefatigable white-washing, and hearth-stoning, and scrubbing and rubbing, could make them. The wonder was, that the brass door- plate, with the interesting inscription 'MRS. TIBBS,' had never caught fire from constant friction, so perseveringly was it polished. There were meat-safe-looking blinds in the parlour- windows, blue and gold curtains in the drawing-room, and spring- roller blinds, as Mrs. Tibbs was won't in the pride of her heart to boast, 'all the way up.' The bell-lamp in the passage looked as clear as a soap-bubble; you could see yourself in all the tables, and

French-polish yourself on any one of the chairs. The banisters were bees-waxed; and the very stair-wires made your eyes wink, they were so glittering.

Mrs. Tibbs was somewhat short of stature, and Mr. Tibbs was by no means a large man. He had, moreover, very short legs, but, by way of indemnification, his face was peculiarly long. He was to his wife what the 0 is in 90, he was of some importance WITH her, he was nothing without her. Mrs. Tibbs was always talking. Mr. Tibbs rarely spoke; but, if it were at any time possible to put in a word, when he should have said nothing at all, he had that talent. Mrs. Tibbs detested long stories, and Mr. Tibbs had one, the conclusion of which had never been heard by his most intimate friends. It always began, 'I recollect when I was in the volunteer corps, in eighteen hundred and six,', but, as he spoke very slowly and softly, and his better half very quickly and loudly, he rarely got beyond the introductory sentence. He was a melancholy specimen of the story-teller. He was the wandering Jew of Joe Millerism.

Mr. Tibbs enjoyed a small independence from the pension-list, about 43l. 15s. 10d. a year. His father, mother, and five interesting scions from the same stock, drew a like sum from the revenue of a grateful country, though for what particular service was never known. But, as this said independence was not quite sufficient to furnish two people with ALL the luxuries of this life, it had occurred to the busy little spouse of Tibbs, that the best thing she could do with a legacy of 700l., would be to take and furnish a tolerable house, somewhere in that partially-explored tract of country which lies between the British Museum, and a remote village called Somers-town, for the reception of boarders. Great Coram- street was the spot pitched upon. The house had been furnished accordingly; two female servants and a boy engaged; and an advertisement inserted in the morning papers, informing the public that 'Six individuals would meet with all the comforts of a cheerful musical home in a select private family, residing within ten minutes' walk of' everywhere. Answers out of number were received, with all sorts of initials; all the letters of the alphabet seemed to be seized with a sudden wish to go out boarding and lodging; voluminous was the correspondence between Mrs. Tibbs and the applicants; and most profound was the secrecy observed. 'E.' didn't like this; 'I.' couldn't think of putting up with that; 'I. O. U.' didn't think the terms would suit him; and 'G. R.' had never slept in a French bed. The result, however, was, that three gentlemen became inmates of Mrs. Tibbs's house, on terms which were 'agreeable to all parties.' In went the advertisement again, and a lady with her two daughters, proposed to increase, not their families, but Mrs. Tibbs's.

'Charming woman, that Mrs. Maplesone!' said Mrs. Tibbs, as she and her spouse were sitting by the fire after breakfast; the gentlemen having gone out on their several avocations. 'Charming woman, indeed!' repeated little Mrs. Tibbs, more by way of soliloquy than anything else, for she never thought of consulting her husband. 'And the two daughters are delightful. We must have some fish to- day; they'll join us at dinner for the first time.'

Mr. Tibbs placed the poker at right angles with the fire shovel, and essayed to speak, but recollected he had nothing to say.

'The young ladies,' continued Mrs. T., 'have kindly volunteered to bring their own piano.'

Tibbs thought of the volunteer story, but did not venture it.

A bright thought struck him -

'It's very likely' said he.

'Pray don't lean your head against the paper,' interrupted Mrs. Tibbs; 'and don't put your feet on the steel fender; that's worse.'

Tibbs took his head from the paper, and his feet from the fender, and proceeded. 'It's very likely one of the young ladies may set her cap at young Mr. Simpson, and you know a marriage'

'A what!' shrieked Mrs. Tibbs. Tibbs modestly repeated his former suggestion.

'I beg you won't mention such a thing,' said Mrs. T. 'A marriage, indeed to rob me c my boarders, no, not for the world.'

Tibbs thought in his own mind that the event was by no means unlikely, but, as he never argued with his wife, he put a stop to the dialogue, by observing it was 'time to go to business.' He always went out at ten o'clock in the morning, and returned a five in the afternoon, with an exceedingly dirty face, and smelling mouldy. Nobody knew what he was, or where he went; but Mrs. Tibbs used to say with an air of grea importance, that he was engaged in the City.

The Miss Maplesones and their accomplished parent arrived in the course of the afternoon in a hackney-coach, and accompanied by a most astonishing number of packages. Trunks, bonnet-boxes, muff- boxes and parasols, guitar-cases, and parcels of all imaginable shapes, done up in brown paper, and fastened with pins, filled the passage. Then, there was such a running up and down with the luggage, such scampering for warm water for the ladies to wash in, and such a bustle, and confusion, and heating of servants, and curling-irons, as had never been known in Great Coram-street before. Little Mrs. Tibbs was quite in her element, bustling about, talking incessantly, and distributing towels and soap, like a head nurse in a hospital. The house was not restored to its usual state of quiet repose, until the ladies were safely shut up in their respective bedrooms, engaged in the important occupation of dressing for dinner.

'Are these gals 'andsome?' inquired Mr. Simpson of Mr. Septimus Hicks, another of the boarders, as they were amusing themselves in the drawing-room, before dinne by lolling on sofas, and contemplating their pumps.

'Don't know,' replied Mr. Septimus Hicks, who was a tallish, white- faced young man, with spectacles, and a black ribbon round his neck instead of a neckerchief, a most interesting person; a poetical walker of the hospitals, and a 'very talented young man.' He was fond of 'lugging' into conversation all sorts of quotations from Don Juan, without fettering himself by the propriety of their application; in which particular he was remarkably independent. The other, Mr. Simpson, was one of those young men, who are in society what walking gentlemen are on the stage, or infinitely worse skilled in his vocation than the most indifferent artist. He was as empty-headed as the great bell of St. Paul's; always dressed according to the caricatures published in the monthly fashion; and spelt Character with a K.

'I saw a devilish number of parcels in the passage when I came home,' simpered Mr. Simpson.

'Materials for the toilet, no doubt,' rejoined the Don Juan reader.

> 'Much linen, lace, and several pair
Of stockings, slippers, brushes, combs, complete;
With other articles of ladies fair,
To keep them beautiful, or leave them neat.'

'Is that from Milton?' inquired Mr. Simpson.

'No, from Byron,' returned Mr. Hicks, with a look of contempt. He was quite sure of his author, because he had never read any other. 'Hush! Here come the gals,' and they both commenced talking in a very loud key.

'Mrs. Maplesone and the Miss Maplesones, Mr. Hicks. Mr. Hicks, Mrs. Maplesone and the Miss Maplesones,' said Mrs. Tibbs, with a very red face, for she had been superintending the cooking operations below stairs, and looked like a wax doll on a sunny day. 'Mr. Simpson, I beg your pardon, Mr. Simpson, Mrs. Maplesone and the Miss Maplesones' and vice versa. The gentlemen immediately began to slide about with much politeness, and to look as if they wished their arms had been legs, so little did they know what to do with them. The ladies smiled, curtseyed, and glided into chairs, and dived for dropped pocket-handkerchiefs: the gentlemen leant against two of the curtain-pegs; Mrs. Tibbs went through an admirable bit of serious pantomime with a servant who had come up to ask some question about the fish-sauce; and then the two young ladies looked at each other; and everybody else appeared to discover something very attractive in the pattern of the fender.

'Julia, my love,' said Mrs. Maplesone to her youngest daughter, in a tone loud enough for the remainder of the company to hear 'Julia.'

'Yes, Ma.'

'Don't stoop.' This was said for the purpose of directing general attention to Miss Julia's figure, which was undeniable. Everybody looked at her, accordingly, and there was another pause.

'We had the most uncivil hackney-coachman to-day, you can imagine,' said Mrs. Maplesone to Mrs. Tibbs, in a confidential tone.

'Dear me!' replied the hostess, with an air of great commiseration. She couldn't say more, for the servant again appeared at the door, and commenced telegraphing most earnestly to her 'Missis.'

'I think hackney-coachmen generally ARE uncivil,' said Mr. Hicks in his most insinuating tone.

'Positively I think they are,' replied Mrs. Maplesone, as if the idea had never struck her before.

'And cabmen, too,' said Mr. Simpson. This remark was a failure, for no one intimated, by word or sign, the slightest knowledge of the manners and customs of cabmen.

'Robinson, what DO you want?' said Mrs. Tibbs to the servant, who, by way of making her presence known to her mistress, had been giving sundry hems and sniffs outside the door during the preceding five minutes.

'Please, ma'am, master wants his clean things,' replied the servant, taken off her guard. The two young men turned their faces to the window, and 'went off' like a couple of bottles of ginger- beer; the ladies put their handkerchiefs to their mouths; and little Mrs. Tibbs bustled out of the room to give Tibbs his clean linen, and the servant warning.

Mr. Calton, the remaining boarder, shortly afterwards made his appearance, and proved a surprising promoter of the conversation. Mr. Calton was a superannuated beau, an old boy. He used to say of himself that although his features were not regularly handsome, they were striking. They certainly were. It was impossible to look at his face without being reminded of a chubby street-door knocker, half-lion half-monkey; and the comparison might be extended to his whole character and conversation. He had stood still, while everything else had been moving. He never originated a conversation, or started an idea; but if any commonplace topic were broached, or, to pursue the comparison, if anybody LIFTED HIM UP, he would hammer away with surprising rapidity. He had the tic- douloureux occasionally, and then he might be said to be muffled, because he did not make quite as much noise as at other times, when he would go on prosing, rat-tat-tat the same thing over and over again. He had never been married; but he was still on the look-out for a wife with money. He had a life interest worth about 300l. a year, he was exceedingly vain, and inordinately selfish. He had acquired the reputation of being the very pink of politeness, and he walked round the park, and up Regent-street, every day.

This respectable personage had made up his mind to render himself exceedingly agreeable to Mrs. Maplesone, indeed, the desire of being as amiable as possible extended itself to the whole party; Mrs. Tibbs having considered it an admirable littl bit of management to represent to the gentlemen that she had SOME reason to believe the ladies were fortunes, and to hint to the ladies, that all the gentlemen were 'eligible.' A little flirtation, she thought, might keep her house full, without leading to any other result.

Mrs. Maplesone was an enterprising widow of about fifty: shrewd, scheming, and good-looking. She was amiably anxious on behalf of her daughters; in proof where she used to remark, that she would have no objection to marry again, if it would benefit her dear girls, she could have no other motive. The 'dear girls' themselves were not at all insensible to the merits of 'a good establishment.' One of them was twenty-five; the other, three years younger. They had been at different watering-places, for four seasons; they had gambled at libraries, read books in balconies, so at fancy fairs, danced at assemblies, talked sentiment, in short, they had done all that industrious girls could do, but, as yet, to no purpose.

'What a magnificent dresser Mr. Simpson is!' whispered Matilda Maplesone to her sister Julia.

'Splendid!' returned the youngest. The magnificent individual alluded to wore a maroon-coloured dress-coat, with a velvet collar and cuffs of the same tint, very like that which usually invests the form of the distinguished unknown who condescends to play the 'swell' in the pantomime at 'Richardson's Show.'

'What whiskers!' said Miss Julia.

'Charming!' responded her sister; 'and what hair!' His hair was like a wig, and distinguished by that insinuating wave which graces the shining locks of those chef-d'oeuvres of art surmounting the waxen images in Bartellot's window in Regent-street; his whiskers meeting beneath his chin, seemed strings wherewith to tie it on, ere science had rendered them unnecessary by her patent invisible springs.

'Dinner's on the table, ma'am, if you please,' said the boy, who now appeared for the first time, in a revived black coat of his master's.

'Oh! Mr. Calton, will you lead Mrs. Maplesone? Thank you.' Mr. Simpson offered his arm to Miss Julia; Mr. Septimus Hicks escorted the lovely Matilda; and the procession proceeded to the dining- room. Mr. Tibbs was introduced, and Mr. Tibbs bobbed up and down to the three ladies like a figure in a Dutch clock, with a powerful spring in the middle of his body, and then dived rapidly into his seat at the bottom of the table, delighted to screen himself behind a soup-tureen, which he could just see over, and that was all. The boarders were seated, a lady and gentleman alternately, like the layers of bread and meat in a plate of sandwiches; and then Mrs. Tibbs directed James to take off the covers. Salmon, lobster- sauce, giblet-soup, and the usual accompaniments were discovered: potatoes like petrifactions, and bits of toasted bread, the shape and size of blank dice.

'Soup for Mrs. Maplesone, my dear,' said the bustling Mrs. Tibbs. She always called her husband 'my dear' before company. Tibbs, who had been eating his bread, and calculating how long it would be before he should get any fish, helped the soup in a hurry, made a small island on the table-cloth, and put his glass upon it, to hide it from his wife.

'Miss Julia, shall I assist you to some fish?'

'If you please, very little, oh! plenty, thank you' (a bit about the size of a walnut put upon the plate).

'Julia is a VERY little eater,' said Mrs. Maplesone to Mr. Calton.

The knocker gave a single rap. He was busy eating the fish with his eyes: so he only ejaculated, 'Ah!'

'My dear,' said Mrs. Tibbs to her spouse after every one else had been helped, 'what will YOU take?' The inquiry was accompanied with a look intimating that he mustn't say fish, because there was not much left. Tibbs thought the frown referred to the island on the table-cloth; he therefore coolly replied, 'Why, I'll take a little- -fish, I think.'

'Did you say fish, my dear?' (another frown).

'Yes, dear,' replied the villain, with an expression of acute hunger depicted in his countenance. The tears almost started to Mrs. Tibbs's eyes, as she helped her 'wretch of a husband,' as she inwardly called him, to the last eatable bit of salmon on the dish.

'James, take this to your master, and take away your master's knife.' This was deliberate revenge, as Tibbs never could eat fish without one. He was, however, constrained to chase small particles of salmon round and round his plate with a piece of bread and a fork, the number of successful attempts being about one in seventeen.

'Take away, James,' said Mrs. Tibbs, as Tibbs swallowed the fourth mouthful, and away went the plates like lightning.

'I'll take a bit of bread, James,' said the poor 'master of the house,' more hungry than ever.

'Never mind your master now, James,' said Mrs. Tibbs, 'see about the meat.' This was conveyed in the tone in which ladies usually give admonitions to servants in company, that is to say, a low one; but which, like a stage whisper, from its peculiar emphasis, is most distinctly heard by everybody present.

A pause ensued, before the table was replenished, a sort of parenthesis in which Mr Simpson, Mr. Calton, and Mr. Hicks, produced respectively a bottle of sauterne, bucellas, and sherry, and took wine with everybody, except Tibbs. No one ever thought of him.

Between the fish and an intimated sirloin, there was a prolonged interval.

Here was an opportunity for Mr. Hicks. He could not resist the singularly appropriate quotation -

'But beef is rare within these oxless isles; Goats' flesh there is, no doubt, and kid, and mutton, And when a holiday upon them smiles, A joint upon their barbarous spits they put on.'

'Very ungentlemanly behaviour,' thought little Mrs. Tibbs, 'to talk in that way.'

'Ah,' said Mr. Calton, filling his glass. 'Tom Moore is my poet.'

'And mine,' said Mrs. Maplesone.

'And mine,' said Miss Julia.

'And mine,' added Mr. Simpson.

Look at his compositions,' resumed the knocker.

To be sure,' said Simpson, with confidence.

Look at Don Juan,' replied Mr. Septimus Hicks.

Julia's letter,' suggested Miss Matilda.

Can anything be grander than the Fire Worshippers?' inquired Miss Julia.

To be sure,' said Simpson.

Or Paradise and the Peri,' said the old beau.

Yes; or Paradise and the Peer,' repeated Simpson, who thought he was getting through it capitally.

It's all very well,' replied Mr. Septimus Hicks, who, as we have before hinted, never had read anything but Don Juan. 'Where will you find anything finer than the description of the siege, at the commencement of the seventh canto?'

Talking of a siege,' said Tibbs, with a mouthful of bread, 'when I was in the volunteer corps, in eighteen hundred and six, our commanding officer was Sir Charles Rampart; and one day, when we were exercising on the ground on which the London University now stands, he says, says he, Tibbs (calling me from the ranks), Tibbs- -'

Tell your master, James,' interrupted Mrs. Tibbs, in an awfully distinct tone, 'tell your master if he WON'T carve those fowls, to send them to me.' The discomfited volunteer instantly set to work, and carved the fowls almost as expeditiously as his wife operated on the haunch of mutton. Whether he ever finished the story is not known but, if he did, nobody heard it.

As the ice was now broken, and the new inmates more at home, every member of the company felt more at ease. Tibbs himself most certainly did, because he went to sleep immediately after dinner. Mr. Hicks and the ladies discoursed most eloquently about poetry, and the theatres, and Lord Chesterfield's Letters; and Mr. Calton followed up what everybody said, with continuous double knocks. Mrs. Tibbs highly approved of every observation that fell from Mrs. Maplesone; and as Mr. Simpson sat with a smile upon his face and said 'Yes,' or 'Certainly,' at intervals of about four minutes each, he received full credit for understanding what was going forward. The gentlemen rejoined the ladies in the drawing-room very shortly after they had left the dining-parlour. Mrs. Maplesone and Mr. Calton played cribbage, and the 'young people' amused themselves with music and conversation. The Miss Maplesones sang the most fascinating duets, and accompanied themselves on guitars, ornamented with bits of ethereal blue ribbon. Mr. Simpson put on a pink waistcoat, and said he was in raptures; and Mr. Hicks felt in the seventh heaven of poetry or the seventh canto of Don Juan, it was the same thing to him. Mrs. Tibbs was quite charmed with the newcomers; and Mr. Tibbs spent the evening in his usual way, he went to sleep, and woke up, and went to sleep again, and woke at supper-time.

* * * * *

We are not about to adopt the licence of novel-writers, and to let 'years roll on;' but we will take the liberty of requesting the reader to suppose that six months have elapsed, since the dinner we have described, and that Mrs. Tibbs's boarders have, during that period, sang, and danced, and gone to theatres and exhibitions, together, as ladies and gentlemen, wherever they board, often do. And we will beg them, the period we have mentioned having elapsed, to imagine farther, that Mr. Septimus Hicks received, in his own bedroom (a front attic), at an early hour one morning, a note from Mr. Calton, requesting the favour of seeing him, as soon as convenient to himself, in his (Calton's) dressing-room on the second-floor back.

'Tell Mr. Calton I'll come down directly,' said Mr. Septimus to the boy. 'Stop, is Mr. Calton unwell?' inquired this excited walker of hospitals, as he put on a bed-furniture-looking dressing-gown.

'Not as I knows on, sir,' replied the boy. ' Please, sir, he looked rather rum, as it might be.'

'Ah, that's no proof of his being ill,' returned Hicks, unconsciously. 'Very well: I'll be down directly.' Downstairs ran the boy with the message, and down went the excited Hicks himself, almost as soon as the message was delivered. 'Tap, tap.' 'Come in.' Door opens, and discovers Mr. Calton sitting in an easy chair. Mutual shakes of the hand exchanged, and Mr. Septimus Hicks motioned to a seat. A short pause. Mr. Hicks coughed, and Mr. Calton took a pinch of snuff. It was one of those interviews where neither party knows what to say. Mr. Septimus Hicks broke silence

'I received a note' he said, very tremulously, in a voice like a Punch with a cold.

'Yes,' returned the other, 'you did.'

'Exactly.'

'Yes.'

Now, although this dialogue must have been satisfactory, both gentlemen felt there was something more important to be said; therefore they did as most men in such situation would have done- -they looked at the table with a determined aspect. The conversation had been opened, however, and Mr. Calton had made up his mind to continue it with a regular double knock. He always spoke very pompously.

'Hicks,' said he, 'I have sent for you, in consequence of certain arrangements which are pending in this house, connected with a marriage.'

'With a marriage!' gasped Hicks, compared with whose expression of countenance, Hamlet's, when he sees his father's ghost, is pleasing and composed.

'With a marriage,' returned the knocker. 'I have sent for you to prove the great confidence I can repose in you.'

And will you betray me?' eagerly inquired Hicks, who in his alarm had even forgotten to quote.

'I betray YOU! Won't YOU betray ME?'

'Never: no one shall know, to my dying day, that you had a hand in the business,' responded the agitated Hicks, with an inflamed countenance, and his hair standing on end as if he were on the stool of an electrifying machine in full operation.

'People must know that, some time or other, within a year, I imagine,' said Mr. Calton, with an air of great self-complacency. 'We MAY have a family.'

'WE! That won't affect you, surely?'

'The devil it won't!'

'No! how can it?' said the bewildered Hicks. Calton was too much inwrapped in the contemplation of his happiness to see the equivoque between Hicks and himself; and threw himself back in his chair. 'Oh, Matilda!' sighed the antique beau, in a lack-a-daisical voice, and applying his right hand a little to the left of the fourth button of his waistcoat, counting from the bottom. 'Oh, Matilda!'

'What Matilda?' inquired Hicks, starting up.

'Matilda Maplesone,' responded the other, doing the same.

'I marry her to-morrow morning,' said Hicks.

'It's false,' rejoined his companion: 'I marry her!'

'You marry her?'

'I marry her!'

'You marry Matilda Maplesone?'

'Matilda Maplesone.'

'MISS Maplesone marry YOU?'

'Miss Maplesone! No; Mrs. Maplesone.'

'Good Heaven!' said Hicks, falling into his chair: 'You marry the mother, and I the daughter!'

'Most extraordinary circumstance!' replied Mr. Calton, 'and rather inconvenient too; for the fact is, that owing to Matilda's wishing to keep her intention secret from her daughters until the ceremony had taken place, she doesn't like applying to any of her friends to give her away. I entertain an objection to making the affair known to any acquaintance just now; and the consequence is, that I sent to you to know whether you'd oblige me by acting as father.'

'I should have been most happy, I assure you,' said Hicks, in a tone of condolence; 'but, you see, I shall be acting as bridegroom. One character is frequently a consequence of the other; but it is not usual to act in both at the same time. There's Simpson, I have no doubt he'll do it for you.'

'I don't like to ask him,' replied Calton, 'he's such a donkey.'

Mr. Septimus Hicks looked up at the ceiling, and down at the floor; at last an idea struck him. 'Let the man of the house, Tibbs, be the father,' he suggested; and then he quoted, as peculiarly applicable to Tibbs and the pair -

'Oh Powers of Heaven! what dark eyes meets she there? "Tis, 'tis her father's, fixed upon the pair.'

'The idea has struck me already,' said Mr. Calton: 'but, you see, Matilda, for what reason I know not, is very anxious that Mrs. Tibbs should know nothing about it, till it's all over. It's a natural delicacy, after all, you know.'

'He's the best-natured little man in existence, if you manage him properly,' said Mr. Septimus Hicks. 'Tell him not to mention it to his wife, and assure him she won't mind it, and he'll do it directly. My marriage is to be a secret one, on account of the mother and MY father; therefore he must be enjoined to secrecy.'

A small double knock, like a presumptuous single one, was that instant heard at the street-door. It was Tibbs; it could be no one else; for no one else occupied five minutes in rubbing his shoes. He had been out to pay the baker's bill.

'Mr. Tibbs,' called Mr. Calton in a very bland tone, looking over the banisters.

'Sir!' replied he of the dirty face.

'Will you have the kindness to step up-stairs for a moment?'

'Certainly, sir,' said Tibbs, delighted to be taken notice of. The bedroom-door was carefully closed, and Tibbs, having put his hat on the floor (as most timid men do), and been accommodated with a seat, looked as astounded as if he were suddenly summoned before the familiars of the Inquisition.

'A rather unpleasant occurrence, Mr. Tibbs,' said Calton, in a very portentous manner, 'obliges me to consult you, and to beg you will not communicate what I am about to say, to your wife.'

Tibbs acquiesced, wondering in his own mind what the deuce the other could have done, and imagining that at least he must have broken the best decanters.

Mr. Calton resumed; 'I am placed, Mr. Tibbs, in rather an unpleasant situation.'

Tibbs looked at Mr. Septimus Hicks, as if he thought Mr. H.'s being in the immediate vicinity of his fellow-boarder might constitute the unpleasantness of his situation; but as he did not exactly know what to say, he merely ejaculated the monosyllable 'Lor!'

'Now,' continued the knocker, 'let me beg you will exhibit no manifestations of surprise, which may be overheard by the domestics, when I tell you, command your feelings of astonishment, that two inmates of this house intend to be married to-morrow morning.' And he drew back his chair, several feet, to perceive the effect of the unlooked-for announcement.

If Tibbs had rushed from the room, staggered down-stairs, and fainted in the passage, if he had instantaneously jumped out of the window into the mews behind the house, in an agony of surprise, his behaviour would have been much less inexplicable to Mr. Calton than it was, when he put his hands into his inexpressible-pockets, and said with a half-chuckle, 'Just so.'

'You are not surprised, Mr. Tibbs?' inquired Mr. Calton.

'Bless you, no, sir,' returned Tibbs; 'after all, its very natural. When two young people get together, you know'

'Certainly, certainly,' said Calton, with an indescribable air of self-satisfaction.

'You don't think it's at all an out-of-the-way affair then?' asked Mr. Septimus Hicks, who had watched the countenance of Tibbs in mute astonishment.

'No, sir,' replied Tibbs; 'I was just the same at his age.' He actually smiled when he said this.

'How devilish well I must carry my years!' thought the delighted old beau, knowing he was at least ten years older than Tibbs at that moment.

'Well, then, to come to the point at once,' he continued, 'I have to ask you whether you will object to act as father on the occasion?'

'Certainly not,' replied Tibbs; still without evincing an atom of surprise.

'You will not?'

'Decidedly not,' reiterated Tibbs, still as calm as a pot of porter with the head off.

Mr. Calton seized the hand of the petticoat-governed little man, and vowed eternal friendship from that hour. Hicks, who was all admiration and surprise, did the same.

'Now, confess,' asked Mr. Calton of Tibbs, as he picked up his hat, 'were you not a little surprised?'

'I b'lieve you!' replied that illustrious person, holding up one hand; 'I b'lieve you! When I first heard of it.'

'So sudden,' said Septimus Hicks.

'So strange to ask ME, you know,' said Tibbs.

'So odd altogether!' said the superannuated love-maker; and then all three laughed.

'I say,' said Tibbs, shutting the door which he had previously opened, and giving full vent to a hitherto corked-up giggle, 'what bothers me is, what WILL his father say?'

Mr. Septimus Hicks looked at Mr. Calton.

'Yes; but the best of it is,' said the latter, giggling in his turn, 'I haven't got a father, he! he! he!'

'You haven't got a father. No; but HE has,' said Tibbs.

'WHO has?' inquired Septimus Hicks.

'Why, HIM.'

'Him, who? Do you know my secret? Do you mean me?'

'You! No; you know who I mean,' returned Tibbs with a knowing wink.

'For Heaven's sake, whom do you mean?' inquired Mr. Calton, who, like Septimus Hicks, was all but out of his senses at the strange confusion.

'Why Mr. Simpson, of course,' replied Tibbs; 'who else could I mean?'

'I see it all,' said the Byron-quoter; 'Simpson marries Julia Maplesone to-morrow morning!'

'Undoubtedly,' replied Tibbs, thoroughly satisfied, 'of course he does.'

It would require the pencil of Hogarth to illustrate, our feeble pen is inadequate to describe, the expression which the countenances of Mr. Calton and Mr. Septimus Hicks respectively assumed, at this unexpected announcement. Equally impossible i it to describe, although perhaps it is easier for our lady readers to imagine, what arts the three ladies could have used, so completely to entangle their separate partners. Whatever they were, however, they were successful. The mother was perfectly aware of the intended marriage of both daughters; and the young ladies were equally acquainted with the intention of their estimable parent. They agreed, however, that it would have a much better appearance if each feigned ignorance of the other's engagement; and it was equally desirable that all the marriages should take place on the same day, to prevent the discovery of one clandestine alliance, operating prejudicially on the others. Hence, the mystification of Mr. Calton and Mr. Septimus Hicks, and the pre-engagement of the unwary Tibbs.

On the following morning, Mr. Septimus Hicks was united to Miss Matilda Maplesone. Mr. Simpson also entered into a 'holy alliance' with Miss Julia; Tibbs acting as father 'his first appearance in that character.' Mr. Calton, not being quite so eager as the two young men, was rather struck by the double discovery; and as he had found some difficulty in getting any one to give the lady away, it occurred to him that the best mode of obviating the inconvenience would be not to take her at all. The lady, however, 'appealed,' as her counsel said on the trial of the cause, Maplesone v. Calton, for a breach of promise, 'with a broken heart, to the outraged laws of her country.' She recovered damages to the amount of 1,000l. which the unfortunate nocker was compelled to pay. Mr. Septimus Hicks having walked the hospitals, took into his head to walk off altogether. His injured wife is at present residing with her mother at Boulogne. Mr. Simpson, having the misfortune to lose his wife six weeks after marriage (by her eloping with an officer during his temporary sojourn in the Fleet Prison, in consequence of his inability to discharge her little mantua-maker's bill), and being disinherited by his father, who died soon afterwards, was fortunate enough to obtain a permanent engagement at a fashionable haircutter's; hairdressing being a science to which he had frequently directed his attention. In this situation he had necessarily many opportunities of making himself acquainted with the habits, and style of thinking, of the exclusive portion of the nobility of this kingdom. To this fortunate circumstance are we indebted for the production of those brilliant efforts of genius, his fashionable novels, which so long as good taste, unsullied by exaggeration, cant, and quackery, continues to exist, cannot fail to instruct and amuse the thinking portion of the community.

only remains to add, that this complication of disorders completely deprived poor Mrs. Tibbs of all her inmates, except the one whom she could have best spared, her husband. That wretched little man returned home, on the day of the wedding, in a state of partial intoxication; and, under the influence of wine, excitement, and despair, actually dared to brave the anger of his wife. Since that ill-fated hour he has constantly taken his meals in the kitchen, to which apartment, it is understood, his witticisms will be in future confined: a turn-up bedstead having been conveyed there by Mrs. Tibbs's order for his exclusive accommodation. It is possible that he will be enabled to finish, in that seclusion, his story of the volunteers.

he advertisement has again appeared in the morning papers. Results must be reserved for another chapter.

## CHAPTER THE SECOND.

'ell!' said little Mrs. Tibbs to herself, as she sat in the front parlour of the Coram-reet mansion one morning, mending a piece of stair-carpet off the first Landings; 'hings have not turned out so badly, either, and if I only get a favourable answer to the advertisement, we shall be full again.'

Mrs. Tibbs resumed her occupation of making worsted lattice-work in the carpet, anxiously listening to the twopenny postman, who was hammering his way down the reet, at the rate of a penny a knock. The house was as quiet as possible. There was only one low sound to be heard, it was the unhappy Tibbs cleaning the gentlemen's boots in the back kitchen, and accompanying himself with a buzzing ise, in wretched mockery of humming a tune.

he postman drew near the house. He paused, so did Mrs. Tibbs. A knock, a bustle, etter, post-paid.

I. presents compt. to I. T. and T. I. begs To say that i see the advertisement And e will Do Herself the pleasure of calling On you at 12 o'clock to-morrow morning.

I. as To apologise to I. T. for the shortness Of the notice But i hope it will not convenience you.

'I remain yours Truly

'Wednesday evening.'

Little Mrs. Tibbs perused the document, over and over again; and the more she read it, the more was she confused by the mixture of the first and third person; the substitution of the 'i' for the 'T. I.;' and the transition from the 'I. T.' to the 'You.' The writing looked like a skein of thread in a tangle, and the note was ingeniously folded into a perfect square, with the direction squeezed up into the right-hand corner, as if it were ashamed of itself. The back of the epistle was pleasingly ornamented with a large red wafer, which, with the addition of divers ink-stains, bore a marvellous resemblance to a black beetle trodden upon. One thing, however, was perfectly clear to the perplexed Mrs. Tibbs. Somebody was to call at twelve. The drawing-room was forthwith dusted for the third time that morning; three or four chairs were pulled out of their places, and a corresponding number of books carefully upset, in order that there might be a due absence of formality. Down went the piece of stair-carpet before noticed, and up ran Mrs. Tibbs 'to make herself tidy.'

The clock of New Saint Pancras Church struck twelve, and the Foundling, with laudable politeness, did the same ten minutes afterwards, Saint something else struck the quarter, and then there arrived a single lady with a double knock, in a pelisse the colour of the interior of a damson pie; a bonnet of the same, with a regular conservatory of artificial flowers; a white veil, and a green parasol, with a cobweb border.

The visitor (who was very fat and red-faced) was shown into the drawing-room; Mrs. Tibbs presented herself, and the negotiation commenced.

'I called in consequence of an advertisement,' said the stranger, in a voice as if she had been playing a set of Pan's pipes for a fortnight without leaving off.

'Yes!' said Mrs. Tibbs, rubbing her hands very slowly, and looking the applicant full in the face, two things she always did on such occasions.

'Money isn't no object whatever to me,' said the lady, 'so much as living in a state of retirement and obtrusion.'

Mrs. Tibbs, as a matter of course, acquiesced in such an exceedingly natural desire.

'I am constantly attended by a medical man,' resumed the pelisse wearer; 'I have been a shocking unitarian for some time, I, indeed, have had very little peace since the death of Mr. Bloss.'

Mrs. Tibbs looked at the relict of the departed Bloss, and thought he must have had very little peace in his time. Of course she could not say so; so she looked very sympathising.

'I shall be a good deal of trouble to you,' said Mrs. Bloss; 'but, for that trouble I am willing to pay. I am going through a course of treatment which renders attention necessary. I have one mutton- chop in bed at half-past eight, and another at ten, every morning.'

Mrs. Tibbs, as in duty bound, expressed the pity she felt for anybody placed in such a distressing situation; and the carnivorous Mrs. Bloss proceeded to arrange the various preliminaries with wonderful despatch. 'Now mind,' said that lady, after terms were arranged; 'I am to have the second-floor front, for my bed-room?'

'Yes, ma'am.'

'And you'll find room for my little servant Agnes?'

'Oh! certainly.'

'And I can have one of the cellars in the area for my bottled porter.'

'With the greatest pleasure; James shall get it ready for you by Saturday.'

'And I'll join the company at the breakfast-table on Sunday morning,' said Mrs. Bloss. 'I shall get up on purpose.'

'Very well,' returned Mrs. Tibbs, in her most amiable tone; for satisfactory references had 'been given and required,' and it was quite certain that the new-comer had plenty of money. 'It's rather singular,' continued Mrs. Tibbs, with what was meant for a most bewitching smile, 'that we have a gentleman now with us, who is in a very delicate state of health, a Mr. Gobler. His apartment is the back drawing-room.'

'The next room?' inquired Mrs. Bloss.

'The next room,' repeated the hostess.

'How very promiscuous!' ejaculated the widow.

'He hardly ever gets up,' said Mrs. Tibbs in a whisper.

'Lor!' cried Mrs. Bloss, in an equally low tone.

'And when he is up,' said Mrs. Tibbs, 'we never can persuade him to go to bed again.'

'Dear me!' said the astonished Mrs. Bloss, drawing her chair nearer Mrs. Tibbs. 'What is his complaint?'

'Why, the fact is,' replied Mrs. Tibbs, with a most communicative air, 'he has no stomach whatever.'

'No what?' inquired Mrs. Bloss, with a look of the most indescribable alarm.

'No stomach,' repeated Mrs. Tibbs, with a shake of the head.

'Lord bless us! what an extraordinary case!' gasped Mrs. Bloss, as if she understood the communication in its literal sense, and was astonished at a gentleman without a stomach finding it necessary to board anywhere.

'When I say he has no stomach,' explained the chatty little Mrs. Tibbs, 'I mean that his digestion is so much impaired, and his interior so deranged, that his stomach is not of the least use to him; in fact, it's an inconvenience.'

'Never heard such a case in my life!' exclaimed Mrs. Bloss. 'Why, he's worse than I am.'

'Oh, yes!' replied Mrs. Tibbs; 'certainly.' She said this with great confidence, for the damson pelisse suggested that Mrs. Bloss, at all events, was not suffering under Mr. Gobler's complaint.

'You have quite incited my curiosity,' said Mrs. Bloss, as she rose to depart. 'How I long to see him!'

'He generally comes down, once a week,' replied Mrs. Tibbs; 'I dare say you'll see him on Sunday.' With this consolatory promise Mrs. Bloss was obliged to be contented. She accordingly walked slowly down the stairs, detailing her complaints all the way; and Mrs. Tibbs followed her, uttering an exclamation of compassion at every step. James (who looked very gritty, for he was cleaning the knives) fell up the kitchen-stairs, and opened the street-door; and, after mutual farewells, Mrs. Bloss slowly departed, down the shady side of the street.

It is almost superfluous to say, that the lady whom we have just shown out at the street-door (and whom the two female servants are now inspecting from the second-floor windows) was exceedingly vulgar, ignorant, and selfish. Her deceased better-half had been an eminent cork-cutter, in which capacity he had amassed a decent fortune. He had no relative but his nephew, and no friend but his cook. The former had the insolence one morning to ask for the loan of fifteen pounds; and, by way of retaliation, he married the latter next day; he made a will immediately afterwards, containing a burst of honest indignation against his nephew (who supported himself and two sisters on 100l. a year), and a bequest of his whole property to his wife. He felt ill after breakfast, and died after dinner. There is a mantelpiece-looking tablet in a civic parish church, setting forth his virtues, and deploring his loss. He never dishonoured a bill, or gave away a halfpenny.

The relict and sole executrix of this noble-minded man was an odd mixture of shrewdness and simplicity, liberality and meanness. Bred up as she had been, she knew no mode of living so agreeable as a boarding-house: and having nothing to do, and nothing to wish for, she naturally imagined she must be ill, an impression which was most assiduously promoted by her medical attendant, Dr. Wosky, and her handmaid Agnes: both of whom, doubtless for good reasons, encouraged all her extravagant notions.

Since the catastrophe recorded in the last chapter, Mrs. Tibbs had been very shy of young-lady boarders. Her present inmates were all lords of the creation, and she availed herself of the opportunity of their assemblage at the dinner-table, to announce the expected arrival of Mrs. Bloss. The gentlemen received the communication with stoical indifference, and Mrs. Tibbs devoted all her energies to prepare for the reception of the valetudinarian. The second- floor front was scrubbed, and washed, and flannelled, till the wet went through to the drawing-room ceiling. Clean white counterpanes, and curtains, and napkins, water-bottles as clea as crystal, blue jugs, and mahogany furniture, added to the splendour, and increased the comfort, of the apartment. The warming-pan was in constant requisition, and a fire lighted in the room every day. The chattels of Mrs. Bloss were forwarded by instalments. First, there came a large hamper of Guinness's stout, and an umbrella; then, a train of trunks; then, a pair of clogs and a bandbox; then, an easy chair with an air-cushion; then, a variety of suspicious- looking packages; and though last not least' Mrs. Bloss and Agnes: the latter in a cherry-coloured merino dress, open-work stockings, and shoes with sandals: like a disguised Columbine.

The installation of the Duke of Wellington, as Chancellor of the University of Oxford, was nothing, in point of bustle and turmoil, to the installation of Mrs. Bloss in her new quarters. True, there was no bright doctor of civil law to deliver a classical address on the occasion; but there were several other old women present, who spoke quite as much to the purpose, and understood themselves equally well. The chop-eater was so fatigued with the process of removal that she declined leaving her room until the following morning; so a mutton-chop, pickle, a pill, a pint bottle of stout, and other medicines, were carried up-stairs for her consumption.

'Why, what DO you think, ma'am?' inquired the inquisitive Agnes of her mistress, after they had been in the house some three hours; 'what DO you think, ma'am? the lady of the house is married.'

'Married!' said Mrs. Bloss, taking the pill and a draught of Guinness, 'married! Impossible!'

'She is indeed, ma'am,' returned the Columbine; 'and her husband, ma'am, lives, he, he, he lives in the kitchen, ma'am.'

'In the kitchen!'

'Yes, ma'am: and he, he, he, the housemaid says, he never goes into the parlour except on Sundays; and that Ms. Tibbs makes him clean the gentlemen's boots; and that he cleans the windows, too, sometimes; and that one morning early, when he was in the front balcony cleaning the drawing-room windows, he called out to a gentleman on the opposite side of the way, who used to live here "Ah! Mr. Calton, Sir, how are you?"' Here the attendant laughed till Mrs. Bloss was in serious apprehension of her chuckling herself into a fit.

'Well, I never!' said Mrs. Bloss.

'Yes. And please, ma'am, the servants gives him gin-and-water sometimes; and then he cries, and says he hates his wife and the boarders, and wants to tickle them.'

'Tickle the boarders!' exclaimed Mrs. Bloss, seriously alarmed.

'No, ma'am, not the boarders, the servants.'

'Oh, is that all!' said Mrs. Bloss, quite satisfied.

'He wanted to kiss me as I came up the kitchen-stairs, just now,' said Agnes, indignantly; 'but I gave it him, a little wretch!'

This intelligence was but too true. A long course of snubbing and neglect; his days spent in the kitchen, and his nights in the turn- up bedstead, had completely broken the little spirit that the unfortunate volunteer had ever possessed. He had no one to whom he could detail his injuries but the servants, and they were almost of necessity his chosen confidants. It is no less strange than true, however, that the little weaknesses which he had incurred, most probably during his military career, seemed to increase as his comforts diminished. He was actually a sort of journeyman Giovanni of the basement story.

The next morning, being Sunday, breakfast was laid in the front parlour at ten o'clock. Nine was the usual time, but the family always breakfasted an hour later on sabbath. Tibbs enrobed himself in his Sunday costume, a black coat, and exceedingly short, thin trousers; with a very large white waistcoat, white stockings and cravat, and Blucher boots, and mounted to the parlour aforesaid. Nobody had come down, and he amused himself by drinking the contents of the milkpot with a teaspoon.

A pair of slippers were heard descending the stairs. Tibbs flew to a chair; and a stern-looking man, of about fifty, with very little hair on his head, and a Sunday paper in his hand, entered the room.

'Good morning, Mr. Evenson,' said Tibbs, very humbly, with something between a nod and a bow.

'How do you do, Mr. Tibbs?' replied he of the slippers, as he sat himself down, and began to read his paper without saying another word.

'Is Mr. Wisbottle in town to-day, do you know, sir?' inquired Tibbs, just for the sake of saying something.

'I should think he was,' replied the stern gentleman. 'He was whistling "The Light Guitar," in the next room to mine, at five o'clock this morning.'

'He's very fond of whistling,' said Tibbs, with a slight smirk.

'Yes, I ain't,' was the laconic reply.

Mr. John Evenson was in the receipt of an independent income, arising chiefly from various houses he owned in the different suburbs. He was very morose and discontented. He was a thorough radical, and used to attend a great variety of pub meetings, for the express purpose of finding fault with everything that was proposed. Mr. Wisbottle, on the other hand, was a high Tory. He was a clerk in the Woods and Forests Office, which he considered rather an aristocratic employment; he knew the peerage by heart, and, could tell you, off-hand, where any illustrious personage lived. He had a good set of teeth, and a capital tailor. Mr. Evenson looked on all these qualifications with profound contempt; and the consequence was that the two were always disputing, much to the edification of the rest of the house. It should be added, that, in addition to his partiality for whistling, Mr. Wisbottle had a

reat idea of his singing powers. There were two other boarders, besides the
entleman in the back drawing-room, Mr. Alfred Tomkins and Mr. Frederick
'Bleary. Mr. Tomkins was a clerk in a wine-house; he was a connoisseur in
aintings, and had a wonderful eye for the picturesque. Mr. O'Bleary was an
rishman, recently imported; he was in a perfectly wild state; and had come over to
ngland to be an apothecary, a clerk in a government office, an actor, a reporter, or
nything else that turned up, he was not particular. He was on familiar terms with
wo small Irish members, and got franks for everybody in the house. He felt
onvinced that his intrinsic merits must procure him a high destiny. He wore
nepherd's-plaid inexpressibles, and used to look under all the ladies' bonnets as he
alked along the streets. His manners and appearance reminded one of Orson.

lere comes Mr. Wisbottle,' said Tibbs; and Mr. Wisbottle forthwith appeared in blue
ippers, and a shawl dressing-gown, whistling 'Di piacer.'

;ood morning, sir,' said Tibbs again. It was almost the only thing he ever said to
nybody

low are you, Tibbs?' condescendingly replied the amateur; and he walked to the
ndow, and whistled louder than ever.

retty air, that!' said Evenson, with a snarl, and without taking his eyes off the
aper.

lad you like it,' replied Wisbottle, highly gratified.

on't you think it would sound better, if you whistled it a little louder?' inquired the
astiff.

o; I don't think it would,' rejoined the unconscious Wisbottle.

I tell you what, Wisbottle,' said Evenson, who had been bottling up his anger for
me hours, 'the next time you feel disposed to whistle "The Light Guitar" at five
:lock in the morning, I'll trouble you to whistle it with your head out o' window. If
u don't, I'll learn the triangle, I will, by'

e entrance of Mrs. Tibbs (with the keys in a little basket) interrupted the threat,
d prevented its conclusion.

's. Tibbs apologised for being down rather late; the bell was rung; James brought
the urn, and received an unlimited order for dry toast and bacon. Tibbs sat down
the bottom of the table, and began eating water-cresses like a Nebuchadnezzar.
. O'Bleary appeared, and Mr. Alfred Tomkins. The compliments of the morning
re exchanged, and the tea was made.

d bless me!' exclaimed Tomkins, who had been looking out at the window. 'Here,
sbottle, pray come here, make haste.'

Wisbottle started from the table, and every one looked up.

'Do you see,' said the connoisseur, placing Wisbottle in the right position, 'a little more this way: there, do you see how splendidly the light falls upon the left side of that broken chimney-pot at No. 48?'

'Dear me! I see,' replied Wisbottle, in a tone of admiration.

'I never saw an object stand out so beautifully against the clear sky in my life,' ejaculated Alfred. Everybody (except John Evenson) echoed the sentiment; for Mr. Tomkins had a great character for finding out beauties which no one else could discover, he certainly deserved it.

'I have frequently observed a chimney-pot in College-green, Dublin, which has a much better effect,' said the patriotic O'Bleary, who never allowed Ireland to be outdone on any point.

The assertion was received with obvious incredulity, for Mr. Tomkins declared that no other chimney-pot in the United Kingdom, broken or unbroken, could be so beautiful as the one at No. 48.

The room-door was suddenly thrown open, and Agnes appeared, leading in Mrs. Bloss, who was dressed in a geranium-coloured muslin gown, and displayed a gold watch of huge dimensions; a chain to match; and a splendid assortment of rings, with enormous stones. A general rush was made for a chair, and a regular introduction took place. Mr. John Evenson made a slight inclination of the head; Mr. Frederick O'Bleary, Mr. Alfred Tomkins, and Mr. Wisbottle, bowed like the mandarins in a grocer's shop; Tibbs rubbed hands, and went round in circles. He was observed to close one eye, and to assume a clock-work sort of expression with the other; this has been considered as a wink, and it has been reported that Agnes was its object. We repel the calumny, and challenge contradiction.

Mrs. Tibbs inquired after Mrs. Bloss's health in a low tone. Mrs. Bloss, with a supreme contempt for the memory of Lindley Murray, answered the various questions in a most satisfactory manner; and a pause ensued, during which the eatables disappeared with awful rapidity.

'You must have been very much pleased with the appearance of the ladies going to the Drawing-room the other day, Mr. O'Bleary?' said Mrs. Tibbs, hoping to start a topic.

'Yes,' replied Orson, with a mouthful of toast.

'Never saw anything like it before, I suppose?' suggested Wisbottle.

'No, except the Lord Lieutenant's levees,' replied O'Bleary.

'Are they at all equal to our drawing-rooms?'

'Oh, infinitely superior!'

Gad! I don't know,' said the aristocratic Wisbottle, 'the Dowager Marchioness of Publiccash was most magnificently dressed, and so was the Baron Slappenbachenhausen.'

What was he presented on?' inquired Evenson.

On his arrival in England.'

I thought so,' growled the radical; 'you never hear of these fellows being presented on their going away again. They know better than that.'

Unless somebody pervades them with an apintment,' said Mrs. Bloss, joining in the conversation in a faint voice.

Well,' said Wisbottle, evading the point, 'it's a splendid sight.'

And did it never occur to you,' inquired the radical, who never would be quiet; 'did it ever occur to you, that you pay for these precious ornaments of society?'

It certainly HAS occurred to me,' said Wisbottle, who thought this answer was a poser; 'it HAS occurred to me, and I am willing to pay for them.'

Well, and it has occurred to me too,' replied John Evenson, 'and I ain't willing to pay for 'em. Then why should I? I say, why should I?' continued the politician, laying down the paper, and knocking his knuckles on the table. 'There are two great principles, demand'

A cup of tea if you please, dear,' interrupted Tibbs.

And supply'

May I trouble you to hand this tea to Mr. Tibbs?' said Mrs. Tibbs, interrupting the argument, and unconsciously illustrating it.

The thread of the orator's discourse was broken. He drank his tea and resumed the paper.

If it's very fine,' said Mr. Alfred Tomkins, addressing the company in general, 'I shall ride down to Richmond to-day, and come back by the steamer. There are some splendid effects of light and shade on the Thames; the contrast between the blueness of the sky and the yellow water is frequently exceedingly beautiful.' Mr. Wisbottle hummed, 'Flow on, thou shining river.'

We have some splendid steam-vessels in Ireland,' said O'Bleary.

Certainly,' said Mrs. Bloss, delighted to find a subject broached in which she could take part.

The accommodations are extraordinary,' said O'Bleary.

'Extraordinary indeed,' returned Mrs. Bloss. 'When Mr. Bloss was alive, he was promiscuously obligated to go to Ireland on business. I went with him, and raly the manner in which the ladies and gentlemen were accommodated with berths, is not creditable.'

Tibbs, who had been listening to the dialogue, looked aghast, and evinced a strong inclination to ask a question, but was checked by a look from his wife. Mr. Wisbottle laughed, and said Tomkins had made a pun; and Tomkins laughed too, and said he had not.

The remainder of the meal passed off as breakfasts usually do. Conversation flagged, and people played with their teaspoons. The gentlemen looked out at the window; walked about the room; and, when they got near the door, dropped off one by one. Tibbs retired to the back parlour by his wife's orders, to check the green-grocer's weekly account; and ultimately Mrs. Tibbs and Mrs. Bloss were left alone together.

'Oh dear!' said the latter, 'I feel alarmingly faint; it's very singular.' (It certainly was for she had eaten four pounds of solids that morning.) 'By-the-bye,' said Mrs. Bloss, 'I have not seen Mr. What's-his-name yet.'

'Mr. Gobler?' suggested Mrs. Tibbs.

'Yes.'

'Oh!' said Mrs. Tibbs, 'he is a most mysterious person. He has his meals regularly sent up-stairs, and sometimes don't leave his room for weeks together.'

'I haven't seen or heard nothing of him,' repeated Mrs. Bloss.

'I dare say you'll hear him to-night,' replied Mrs. Tibbs; 'he generally groans a good deal on Sunday evenings.'

'I never felt such an interest in any one in my life,' ejaculated Mrs. Bloss. A little double-knock interrupted the conversation; Dr. Wosky was announced, and duly shown in. He was a little man with a red face, dressed of course in black, with a stiff white neckerchief. He had a very good practice, and plenty of money, which he had amassed by invariably humouring the worst fancies of all the females of all the families he had ever been introduced into. Mrs. Tibbs offered to retire, but was entreated to stay.

'Well, my dear ma'am, and how are we?' inquired Wosky, in a soothing tone.

'Very ill, doctor, very ill,' said Mrs. Bloss, in a whisper

'Ah! we must take care of ourselves; we must, indeed,' said the obsequious Wosky as he felt the pulse of his interesting patient.

'How is our appetite?'

Mrs. Bloss shook her head.

'Our friend requires great care,' said Wosky, appealing to Mrs. Tibbs, who of course assented. 'I hope, however, with the blessing of Providence, that we shall be enabled to make her quite stout again.' Mrs. Tibbs wondered in her own mind what the patient would be when she was made quite stout.

We must take stimulants,' said the cunning Wosky, 'plenty of nourishment, and, above all, we must keep our nerves quiet; we positively must not give way to our sensibilities. We must take all we can get,' concluded the doctor, as he pocketed his fee, 'and we must keep quiet.'

Dear man!' exclaimed Mrs. Bloss, as the doctor stepped into the carriage.

Charming creature indeed, quite a lady's man!' said Mrs. Tibbs, and Dr. Wosky rattled away to make fresh gulls of delicate females, and pocket fresh fees.

As we had occasion, in a former paper, to describe a dinner at Mrs. Tibbs's; and as one meal went off very like another on all ordinary occasions; we will not fatigue our readers by entering into any other detailed account of the domestic economy of the establishment. We will therefore proceed to events, merely premising that the mysterious tenant of the back drawing-room was a lazy, selfish hypochondriac; always complaining and never ill. As his character in many respects closely assimilated to that of Mrs. Bloss, a very warm friendship soon sprung up between them. He was tall, thin, and pale; he always fancied he had a severe pain somewhere or other, and his face invariably wore a pinched, screwed-up expression; he looked, indeed, like a man who had got his feet in a tub of exceedingly hot water, against his will.

For two or three months after Mrs. Bloss's first appearance in Coram-street, John Evenson was observed to become, every day, more sarcastic and more ill-natured; and there was a degree of additional importance in his manner, which clearly showed that he fancied he had discovered something, which he only wanted a proper opportunity of divulging. He found it at last.

One evening, the different inmates of the house were assembled in the drawing-room engaged in their ordinary occupations. Mr. Gobler and Mrs. Bloss were sitting at a small card-table near the centre window, playing cribbage; Mr. Wisbottle was describing semicircles on the music-stool, turning over the leaves of a book on the piano, and humming most melodiously; Alfred Tomkins was sitting at the round table, with his elbows duly squared, making a pencil sketch of a head considerably larger than his own; O'Bleary was reading Horace, and trying to look as if he understood it; and John Evenson had drawn his chair close to Mrs. Tibbs's work-table, and was talking to her very earnestly in a low tone.

I can assure you, Mrs. Tibbs,' said the radical, laying his forefinger on the muslin she was at work on; 'I can assure you, Mrs. Tibbs, that nothing but the interest I take in your welfare would induce me to make this communication. I repeat, I fear Wisbottle is endeavouring to gain the affections of that young woman, Agnes, and that he is in the habit of meeting her in the store-room on the first floor, over the heads. From my bedroom I distinctly heard voices there, last night. I opened my door immediately, and crept very softly on to the landing; there I saw Mr. Tibbs, who, it seems, had been disturbed also. Bless me, Mrs. Tibbs, you change colour!'

'No, no, it's nothing,' returned Mrs. T. in a hurried manner; 'it's only the heat of the room.'

'A flush!' ejaculated Mrs. Bloss from the card-table; 'that's good for four.'

'If I thought it was Mr. Wisbottle,' said Mrs. Tibbs, after a pause, 'he should leave this house instantly.'

'Go!' said Mrs. Bloss again.

'And if I thought,' continued the hostess with a most threatening air, 'if I thought he was assisted by Mr. Tibbs'

'One for his nob!' said Gobler.

'Oh,' said Evenson, in a most soothing tone, he liked to make mischief, 'I should hope Mr. Tibbs was not in any way implicated. He always appeared to me very harmless.'

'I have generally found him so,' sobbed poor little Mrs. Tibbs; crying like a watering-pot.

'Hush! hush! pray, Mrs. Tibbs, consider, we shall be observed, pray, don't!' said John Evenson, fearing his whole plan would be interrupted. 'We will set the matter at rest with the utmost care, and I shall be most happy to assist you in doing so.' Mrs. Tibbs murmured her thanks.

'When you think every one has retired to rest to-night,' said Evenson very pompously, 'if you'll meet me without a light, just outside my bedroom door, by the staircase window, I think we can ascertain who the parties really are, and you will afterwards be enabled to proceed as you think proper.'

Mrs. Tibbs was easily persuaded; her curiosity was excited, her jealousy was roused and the arrangement was forthwith made. She resumed her work, and John Evenson walked up and down the room with his hands in his pockets, looking as if nothing had happened. The game of cribbage was over, and conversation began again.

'Well, Mr. O'Bleary,' said the humming-top, turning round on his pivot, and facing the company, 'what did you think of Vauxhall the other night?'

'Oh, it's very fair,' replied Orson, who had been enthusiastically delighted with the whole exhibition.

'Never saw anything like that Captain Ross's set-out, eh?'

'No,' returned the patriot, with his usual reservation, 'except in Dublin.'

'I saw the Count de Canky and Captain Fitzthompson in the Gardens,' said Wisbottle; 'they appeared much delighted.'

'Then it MUST be beautiful,' snarled Evenson.

think the white bears is partickerlerly well done,' suggested Mrs. Bloss. 'In their shaggy white coats, they look just like Polar bears, don't you think they do, Mr. Evenson?'

'think they look a great deal more like omnibus cads on all fours,' replied the discontented one.

'Upon the whole, I should have liked our evening very well,' gasped Gobler; 'only I caught a desperate cold which increased my pain dreadfully! I was obliged to have several shower-baths, before I could leave my room.'

'Capital things those shower-baths!' ejaculated Wisbottle.

'Excellent!' said Tomkins.

'Delightful!' chimed in O'Bleary. (He had once seen one, outside a tinman's.)

'Disgusting machines!' rejoined Evenson, who extended his dislike to almost every created object, masculine, feminine, or neuter.

'Disgusting, Mr. Evenson!' said Gobler, in a tone of strong indignation. 'Disgusting! Look at their utility, consider how many lives they have saved by promoting perspiration.'

'Promoting perspiration, indeed,' growled John Evenson, stopping short in his walk across the large squares in the pattern of the carpet, 'I was ass enough to be persuaded some time ago to have one in my bedroom. 'Gad, I was in it once, and it effectually cured ME, for the mere sight of it threw me into a profuse perspiration for six months afterwards.'

A titter followed this announcement, and before it had subsided James brought up the tray,' containing the remains of a leg of lamb which had made its debut at dinner; bread; cheese; an atom of butter in a forest of parsley; one pickled walnut and the third of another; and so forth. The boy disappeared, and returned again with another tray, containing glasses and jugs of hot and cold water. The gentlemen brought in their spirit-bottles; the housemaid placed divers plated bedroom candlesticks under the card-table; and the servants retired for the night.

Chairs were drawn round the table, and the conversation proceeded in the customary manner. John Evenson, who never ate supper, lolled on the sofa, and amused himself by contradicting everybody. O'Bleary ate as much as he could conveniently carry, and Mrs. Tibbs felt a due degree of indignation thereat; Mr. Gobler and Mrs. Bloss conversed most affectionately on the subject of pill-taking, and other innocent amusements; and Tomkins and Wisbottle 'got into an argument;' that is to say, they both talked very loudly and vehemently, each flattering himself that he had got some advantage about something, and neither of them having more than a very indistinct idea of what they were talking about. An hour or two passed away; and the boarders and the plated candlesticks retired in pairs to their respective bedrooms. John Evenson pulled off his boots, locked his door, and determined to sit up until Mr. Gobler had retired. He always sat in the drawing-room an hour after everybody else had left it, taking medicine, and groaning.

Great Coram-street was hushed into a state of profound repose: it was nearly two o'clock. A hackney-coach now and then rumbled slowly by; and occasionally some stray lawyer's clerk, on his way home to Somers-town, struck his iron heel on the top of the coal- cellar with a noise resembling the click of a smoke-Jack. A low, monotonous, gushing sound was heard, which added considerably to the romantic dreariness of the scene. It was the water 'coming in' at number eleven.

'He must be asleep by this time,' said John Evenson to himself, after waiting with exemplary patience for nearly an hour after Mr. Gobler had left the drawing-room. He listened for a few moments; the house was perfectly quiet; he extinguished his rushlight, and opened his bedroom door. The staircase was so dark that it was impossible to see anything.

'S-s-s!' whispered the mischief-maker, making a noise like the first indication a catherine-wheel gives of the probability of its going off.

'Hush!' whispered somebody else.

'Is that you, Mrs. Tibbs?'

'Yes, sir.'

'Where?'

'Here;' and the misty outline of Mrs. Tibbs appeared at the staircase window, like the ghost of Queen Anne in the tent scene in Richard.

'This way, Mrs. Tibbs,' whispered the delighted busybody: 'give me your hand, there! Whoever these people are, they are in the store- room now, for I have been looking down from my window, and I could see that they accidentally upset their candlestick, and are now in darkness. You have no shoes on, have you?'

'No,' said little Mrs. Tibbs, who could hardly speak for trembling.

'Well; I have taken my boots off, so we can go down, close to the store-room door, and listen over the banisters;' and down-stairs they both crept accordingly, every board creaking like a patent mangle on a Saturday afternoon.

'It's Wisbottle and somebody, I'll swear,' exclaimed the radical in an energetic whisper, when they had listened for a few moments.

'Hush, pray let's hear what they say!' exclaimed Mrs. Tibbs, the gratification of whose curiosity was now paramount to every other consideration.

'Ah! if I could but believe you,' said a female voice coquettishly, 'I'd be bound to settle my missis for life.'

'What does she say?' inquired Mr. Evenson, who was not quite so well situated as his companion.

She says she'll settle her missis's life,' replied Mrs. Tibbs. 'The wretch! they're plotting murder.'

I know you want money,' continued the voice, which belonged to Agnes; 'and if you'd secure me the five hundred pound, I warrant she should take fire soon enough.'

What's that?' inquired Evenson again. He could just hear enough to want to hear more.

I think she says she'll set the house on fire,' replied the affrighted Mrs. Tibbs. 'But thank God I'm insured in the Phoenix!'

The moment I have secured your mistress, my dear,' said a man's voice in a strong Irish brogue, 'you may depend on having the money.'

Bless my soul, it's Mr. O'Bleary!' exclaimed Mrs. Tibbs, in a parenthesis.

The villain!' said the indignant Mr. Evenson.

The first thing to be done,' continued the Hibernian, 'is to poison Mr. Gobler's mind.'

Oh, certainly,' returned Agnes.

What's that?' inquired Evenson again, in an agony of curiosity and a whisper.

He says she's to mind and poison Mr. Gobler,' replied Mrs. Tibbs, aghast at this sacrifice of human life.

And in regard of Mrs. Tibbs,' continued O'Bleary. Mrs. Tibbs shuddered.

Hush!' exclaimed Agnes, in a tone of the greatest alarm, just as Mrs. Tibbs was on the extreme verge of a fainting fit. 'Hush!'

Hush!' exclaimed Evenson, at the same moment to Mrs. Tibbs.

There's somebody coming UP-stairs,' said Agnes to O'Bleary.

There's somebody coming DOWN-stairs,' whispered Evenson to Mrs. Tibbs.

Go into the parlour, sir,' said Agnes to her companion. 'You will get there, before whoever it is, gets to the top of the kitchen stairs.'

The drawing-room, Mrs. Tibbs!' whispered the astonished Evenson to his equally astonished companion; and for the drawing-room they both made, plainly hearing the rustling of two persons, one coming down-stairs, and one coming up.

What can it be?' exclaimed Mrs. Tibbs. 'It's like a dream. I wouldn't be found in this situation for the world!'

'Nor I,' returned Evenson, who could never bear a joke at his own expense. 'Hush! here they are at the door.'

'What fun!' whispered one of the new-comers. It was Wisbottle.

'Glorious!' replied his companion, in an equally low tone. This was Alfred Tomkins. 'Who would have thought it?'

'I told you so,' said Wisbottle, in a most knowing whisper. 'Lord bless you, he has paid her most extraordinary attention for the last two months. I saw 'em when I was sitting at the piano to- night.'

'Well, do you know I didn't notice it?' interrupted Tomkins.

'Not notice it!' continued Wisbottle. 'Bless you; I saw him whispering to her, and she crying; and then I'll swear I heard him say something about to-night when we were all in bed.'

'They're talking of US!' exclaimed the agonised Mrs. Tibbs, as the painful suspicion, and a sense of their situation, flashed upon her mind.

'I know it, I know it,' replied Evenson, with a melancholy consciousness that there was no mode of escape.

'What's to be done? we cannot both stop here!' ejaculated Mrs. Tibbs, in a state of partial derangement.

'I'll get up the chimney,' replied Evenson, who really meant what he said.

'You can't,' said Mrs. Tibbs, in despair. 'You can't, it's a register stove.'

'Hush!' repeated John Evenson.

'Hush, hush!' cried somebody down-stairs.

'What a d-d hushing!' said Alfred Tomkins, who began to get rather bewildered.

'There they are!' exclaimed the sapient Wisbottle, as a rustling noise was heard in the store-room.

'Hark!' whispered both the young men.

'Hark!' repeated Mrs. Tibbs and Evenson.

'Let me alone, sir,' said a female voice in the store-room.

'Oh, Hagnes!' cried another voice, which clearly belonged to Tibbs, for nobody else ever owned one like it, 'Oh, Hagnes, lovely creature!'

'Be quiet, sir!' (A bounce.)

'Hag'

'Be quiet, sir, I am ashamed of you. Think of your wife, Mr. Tibbs. Be quiet, sir!'

My wife!' exclaimed the valorous Tibbs, who was clearly under the influence of gin-and-water, and a misplaced attachment; 'I ate her! Oh, Hagnes! when I was in the volunteer corps, in eighteen hundred and'

I declare I'll scream. Be quiet, sir, will you?' (Another bounce and a scuffle.)

What's that?' exclaimed Tibbs, with a start.

What's what?' said Agnes, stopping short.

Why that!'

Ah! you have done it nicely now, sir,' sobbed the frightened Agnes, as a tapping was heard at Mrs. Tibbs's bedroom door, which would have beaten any dozen woodpeckers hollow.

Mrs. Tibbs! Mrs. Tibbs!' called out Mrs. Bloss. 'Mrs. Tibbs, pray get up.' (Here the imitation of a woodpecker was resumed with tenfold violence.)

Oh, dear, dear!' exclaimed the wretched partner of the depraved Tibbs. 'She's knocking at my door. We must be discovered! What will they think?'

Mrs. Tibbs! Mrs. Tibbs!' screamed the woodpecker again.

What's the matter!' shouted Gobler, bursting out of the back drawing-room, like the dragon at Astley's.

Oh, Mr. Gobler!' cried Mrs. Bloss, with a proper approximation to hysterics; 'I think the house is on fire, or else there's thieves in it. I have heard the most dreadful noises!'

The devil you have!' shouted Gobler again, bouncing back into his den, in happy imitation of the aforesaid dragon, and returning immediately with a lighted candle. Why, what's this? Wisbottle! Tomkins! O'Bleary! Agnes! What the deuce! all up and dressed?'

Astonishing!' said Mrs. Bloss, who had run down-stairs, and taken Mr. Gobler's arm.

Call Mrs. Tibbs directly, somebody,' said Gobler, turning into the front drawing-room. 'What! Mrs. Tibbs and Mr. Evenson!!'

Mrs. Tibbs and Mr. Evenson!' repeated everybody, as that unhappy pair were discovered: Mrs. Tibbs seated in an arm-chair by the fireplace, and Mr. Evenson standing by her side,

We must leave the scene that ensued to the reader's imagination. We could tell, how Mrs. Tibbs forthwith fainted away, and how it required the united strength of Mr.

Wisbottle and Mr. Alfred Tomkins to hold her in her chair; how Mr. Evenson explained, and how his explanation was evidently disbelieved; how Agnes repelled the accusations of Mrs. Tibbs by proving that she was negotiating with Mr. O'Bleary to influence her mistress's affections in his behalf; and how Mr. Gobler threw a damp counterpane on the hopes of Mr. O'Bleary by avowing that he (Gobler) had already proposed to, and been accepted by, Mrs. Bloss; how Agnes was discharged from that lady's service; how Mr. O'Bleary discharged himself from Mrs. Tibbs's house, without going through the form of previously discharging his bill; and how that disappointed young gentleman rails against England and the English, and vows there is no virtue or fine feeling extant, 'except in Ireland.' We repeat that we COULD tell all this, but we love to exercise our self-denial, and we therefore prefer leaving it to be imagined.

The lady whom we have hitherto described as Mrs. Bloss, is no more. Mrs. Gobler exists: Mrs. Bloss has left us for ever. In a secluded retreat in Newington Butts, far, far removed from the noisy strife of that great boarding-house, the world, the enviable Gobler and his pleasing wife revel in retirement: happy in their complaints, their table, and their medicine, wafted through life by the grateful prayers of all the purveyors of animal food within three miles round.

We would willingly stop here, but we have a painful duty imposed upon us, which we must discharge. Mr. and Mrs. Tibbs have separated by mutual consent, Mrs. Tibbs receiving one moiety of 43l. 15s. 10d., which we before stated to be the amount of her husband's annual income, and Mr. Tibbs the other. He is spending the evening of his days in retirement; and he is spending also, annually, that small but honourable independence. He resides among the original settlers at Walworth; and it has been stated, on unquestionable authority, that the conclusion of the volunteer story has been heard in a small tavern in that respectable neighbourhood.

The unfortunate Mrs. Tibbs has determined to dispose of the whole of her furniture by public auction, and to retire from a residence in which she has suffered so much. Mr. Robins has been applied to, to conduct the sale, and the transcendent abilities of the literary gentlemen connected with his establishment are now devoted to the task of drawing up the preliminary advertisement. It is to contain, among a variety of brilliant matter, seventy-eight words in large capitals, and six original quotations in inverted commas.

# The Lamplighter

'If you talk of Murphy and Francis Moore, gentlemen,' said the lamplighter who was in the chair, 'I mean to say that neither of 'em ever had any more to do with the stars than Tom Grig had.'

'And what had HE to do with 'em?' asked the lamplighter who officiated as vice.

'Nothing at all,' replied the other; 'just exactly nothing at all.'

'Do you mean to say you don't believe in Murphy, then?' demanded the lamplighter who had opened the discussion.

'I mean to say I believe in Tom Grig,' replied the chairman. 'Whether I believe in Murphy, or not, is a matter between me and my conscience; and whether Murphy believes in himself, or not, is a matter between him and his conscience. Gentlemen, I drink your healths.'

The lamplighter who did the company this honour, was seated in the chimney-corner of a certain tavern, which has been, time out of mind, the Lamplighters' House of Call. He sat in the midst of a circle of lamplighters, and was the cacique, or chief of the tribe.

If any of our readers have had the good fortune to behold a lamplighter's funeral, they will not be surprised to learn that lamplighters are a strange and primitive people; that they rigidly adhere to old ceremonies and customs which have been handed down among them from father to son since the first public lamp was lighted out of doors; that they intermarry, and betroth their children in infancy; that they enter into no plots or conspiracies (for who ever heard of a traitorous lamplighter?); that they commit no crimes against the laws of their country (there being no instance of a murderous or burglarious lamplighter); that they are, in short, notwithstanding their apparently volatile and restless character, a highly moral and reflective people: having among themselves as many traditional observances as the Jews, and being, as a body, if not as old as the hills, at least as old as the streets. It is an article of their creed that the first faint glimmering of true civilisation shone in the first street-light maintained at the public expense. They trace their existence and high position in the public esteem, in a direct line to the heathen mythology; and hold that the history of Prometheus himself is but a pleasant fable, whereof the true hero is a lamplighter.

'Gentlemen,' said the lamplighter in the chair, 'I drink your healths.'

'And perhaps, Sir,' said the vice, holding up his glass, and rising a little way off his seat and sitting down again, in token that he recognised and returned the compliment, 'perhaps you will add to that condescension by telling us who Tom Grig was, and how he came to be connected in your mind with Francis Moore, Physician.'

'Hear, hear, hear!' cried the lamplighters generally.

'Tom Grig, gentlemen,' said the chairman, 'was one of us; and it happened to him, as it don't often happen to a public character in our line, that he had his what-you-may-call-it cast.'

'His head?' said the vice.

'No,' replied the chairman, 'not his head.'

'His face, perhaps?' said the vice. 'No, not his face.' 'His legs?' 'No, not his legs.' Nor yet his arms, nor his hands, nor his feet, nor his chest, all of which were severally suggested.

'His nativity, perhaps?'

'That's it,' said the chairman, awakening from his thoughtful attitude at the suggestion. 'His nativity. That's what Tom had cast, gentlemen.'

'In plaster?' asked the vice.

'I don't rightly know how it's done,' returned the chairman. 'But I suppose it was.'

And there he stopped as if that were all he had to say; whereupon there arose a murmur among the company, which at length resolved itself into a request, conveyed through the vice, that he would go on. This being exactly what the chairman wanted, he mused for a little time, performed that agreeable ceremony which is popularly termed wetting one's whistle, and went on thus:

'Tom Grig, gentlemen, was, as I have said, one of us; and I may go further, and say he was an ornament to us, and such a one as only the good old times of oil and cotton could have produced. Tom's family, gentlemen, were all lamplighters.'

'Not the ladies, I hope?' asked the vice.

'They had talent enough for it, Sir,' rejoined the chairman, 'and would have been, but for the prejudices of society. Let women have their rights, Sir, and the females of Tom's family would have been every one of 'em in office. But that emancipation hasn't come yet, and hadn't then, and consequently they confined themselves to the bosoms of their families, cooked the dinners, mended the clothes, minded the children, comforted their husbands, and attended to the house-keeping generally. It's a hard thing upon the women, gentlemen, that they are limited to such a sphere of action as this; very hard.

'I happen to know all about Tom, gentlemen, from the circumstance of his uncle by his mother's side, having been my particular friend. His (that's Tom's uncle's) fate was a melancholy one. Gas was the death of him. When it was first talked of, he laughed. He wasn't angry; he laughed at the credulity of human nature. "They might as well talk," he says, "of laying on an everlasting succession of glow-worms;" and then he laughed again, partly at his joke, and partly at poor humanity.

'In course of time, however, the thing got ground, the experiment was made, and they lighted up Pall Mall. Tom's uncle went to see it. I've heard that he fell off his ladder fourteen times that night, from weakness, and that he would certainly have gone on falling till he killed himself, if his last tumble hadn't been into a wheelbarrow which was going his way, and humanely took him home. "I foresee in this," says Tom's uncle faintly, and taking to his bed as he spoke - "I foresee in this," he says "the breaking up of our profession. There's no more going the rounds to trim by daylight, no more dribbling down of the oil on the hats and bonnets of ladies and gentlemen when one feels in spirits. Any low fellow can light a gas-lamp. And it's all up." In this state of mind, he petitioned the government for - I want a word again, gentlemen - what do you call that which they give to people when it's found out, at last, that they've never been of any use, and have been paid too much for doing nothing?'

Compensation?' suggested the vice.

That's it,' said the chairman. 'Compensation. They didn't give it him, though, and hen he got very fond of his country all at once, and went about saying that gas was a death-blow to his native land, and that it was a plot of the radicals to ruin the country and destroy the oil and cotton trade for ever, and that the whales would go and kill themselves privately, out of sheer spite and vexation at not being caught. At ast he got right-down cracked; called his tobacco-pipe a gas-pipe; thought his tears vere lamp- oil; and went on with all manner of nonsense of that sort, till one night ie hung himself on a lamp-iron in Saint Martin's Lane, and there was an end of HIM.

Tom loved him, gentlemen, but he survived it. He shed a tear over his grave, got ery drunk, spoke a funeral oration that night in the watch-house, and was fined five hillings for it, in the morning. Some men are none the worse for this sort of thing. om was one of 'em. He went that very afternoon on a new beat: as clear in his ead, and as free from fever as Father Mathew himself.

Tom's new beat, gentlemen, was - I can't exactly say where, for that he'd never ell; but I know it was in a quiet part of town, where there were some queer old ouses. I have always had it in my head that it must have been somewhere near Canonbury Tower in Islington, but that's a matter of opinion. Wherever it was, he ent upon it, with a bran-new ladder, a white hat, a brown holland jacket and rousers, a blue neck-kerchief, and a sprig of full- blown double wall-flower in his utton-hole. Tom was always genteel in his appearance, and I have heard from the est judges, that if he had left his ladder at home that afternoon, you might have ook him for a lord.

le was always merry, was Tom, and such a singer, that if there was any ncouragement for native talent, he'd have been at the opera. He was on his ladder, ghting his first lamp, and singing to himself in a manner more easily to be onceived than described, when he hears the clock strike five, and suddenly sees an d gentleman with a telescope in his hand, throw up a window and look at him very ard.

om didn't know what could be passing in this old gentleman's mind. He thought it ely enough that he might be saying within himself, "Here's a new lamplighter - a ood-looking young fellow - shall I stand something to drink?" Thinking this ssible, he keeps quite still, pretending to be very particular about the wick, and oks at the old gentleman sideways, seeming to take no notice of him.

entlemen, he was one of the strangest and most mysterious-looking files that ever m clapped his eyes on. He was dressed all slovenly and untidy, in a great gown of kind of bed-furniture pattern, with a cap of the same on his head; and a long old pped waistcoat; with no braces, no strings, very few buttons - in short, with rdly any of those artificial contrivances that hold society together. Tom knew by ese signs, and by his not being shaved, and by his not being over-clean, and by a rt of wisdom not quite awake, in his face, that he was a scientific old gentleman. e often told me that if he could have conceived the possibility of the whole Royal ociety being boiled down into one man, he should have said the old gentleman's dy was that Body.

'The old gentleman claps the telescope to his eye, looks all round, sees nobody else in sight, stares at Tom again, and cries out very loud:

'"Hal-loa!"

'"Halloa, Sir," says Tom from the ladder; "and halloa again, if you come to that."

'"Here's an extraordinary fulfilment," says the old gentleman, "of a prediction of the planets."

'"Is there?" says Tom. "I'm very glad to hear it."

'"Young man," says the old gentleman, "you don't know me."

'"Sir," says Tom, "I have not that honour; but I shall be happy to drink your health, notwithstanding."

'"I read," cries the old gentleman, without taking any notice of this politeness on Tom's part - "I read what's going to happen, in the stars."

'Tom thanked him for the information, and begged to know if anything particular was going to happen in the stars, in the course of a week or so; but the old gentleman, correcting him, explained that he read in the stars what was going to happen on dry land, and that he was acquainted with all the celestial bodies.

'"I hope they're all well, Sir," says Tom, - "everybody."

'"Hush!" cries the old gentleman. "I have consulted the book of Fate with rare and wonderful success. I am versed in the great sciences of astrology and astronomy. In my house here, I have every description of apparatus for observing the course and motion of the planets. Six months ago, I derived from this source, the knowledge that precisely as the clock struck five this afternoon a stranger would present himself - the destined husband of my young and lovely niece - in reality of illustrious and high descent, but whose birth would be enveloped in uncertainty and mystery. Don't tell me yours isn't," says the old gentleman, who was in such a hurry to speak that he couldn't get the words out fast enough, "for I know better."

'Gentlemen, Tom was so astonished when he heard him say this, that he could hardly keep his footing on the ladder, and found it necessary to hold on by the lamp-post. There WAS a mystery about his birth. His mother had always admitted it. Tom had never known who was his father, and some people had gone so far as to say that even SHE was in doubt.

'While he was in this state of amazement, the old gentleman leaves the window, bursts out of the house-door, shakes the ladder, and Tom, like a ripe pumpkin, comes sliding down into his arms.

'"Let me embrace you," he says, folding his arms about him, and nearly lighting up his old bed-furniture gown at Tom's link. "You're a man of noble aspect. Everything combines to prove the accuracy of my observations. You have had mysterious promptings within you," he says; "I know you have had whisperings of greatness, eh?" he says.

"I think I have," says Tom - Tom was one of those who can persuade themselves to anything they like - "I've often thought I wasn't the small beer I was taken for."

"You were right," cries the old gentleman, hugging him again. "Come in. My niece awaits us."

"Is the young lady tolerable good-looking, Sir?" says Tom, hanging fire rather, as he thought of her playing the piano, and knowing French, and being up to all manner of accomplishments.

"She's beautiful!" cries the old gentleman, who was in such a terrible bustle that he was all in a perspiration. "She has a graceful carriage, an exquisite shape, a sweet voice, a countenance beaming with animation and expression; and the eye," he says, rubbing his hands, "of a startled fawn."

Tom supposed this might mean, what was called among his circle of acquaintance, a game eye;" and, with a view to this defect, inquired whether the young lady had any cash.

'She has five thousand pounds," cries the old gentleman. "But what of that? what of that? A word in your ear. I'm in search of the philosopher's stone. I have very nearly found it - not quite. It turns everything to gold; that's its property."

Tom naturally thought it must have a deal of property; and said that when the old gentleman did get it, he hoped he'd be careful to keep it in the family.

Certainly," he says, "of course. Five thousand pounds! What's five thousand pounds to us? What's five million?" he says. "What's five thousand million? Money will be nothing to us. We shall never be able to spend it fast enough."

We'll try what we can do, Sir," says Tom.

We will," says the old gentleman. "Your name?"

Grig," says Tom.

The old gentleman embraced him again, very tight; and without speaking another word, dragged him into the house in such an excited manner, that it was as much as Tom could do to take his link and ladder with him, and put them down in the passage.

Gentlemen, if Tom hadn't been always remarkable for his love of truth, I think you would still have believed him when he said that all this was like a dream. There is no better way for a man to find out whether he is really asleep or awake, than calling for something to eat. If he's in a dream, gentlemen, he'll find something wanting in flavour, depend upon it.

'Tom explained his doubts to the old gentleman, and said that if there was any cold meat in the house, it would ease his mind very much to test himself at once. The old gentleman ordered up a venison pie, a small ham, and a bottle of very old Madeira. At the first mouthful of pie and the first glass of wine, Tom smacks his lips and cries out, "I'm awake - wide awake;" and to prove that he was so, gentlemen, he made an end of 'em both.

'When Tom had finished his meal (which he never spoke of afterwards without tears in his eyes), the old gentleman hugs him again, and says, "Noble stranger! let us visit my young and lovely niece." Tom, who was a little elevated with the wine, replies, "The noble stranger is agreeable!" At which words the old gentleman took him by the hand, and led him to the parlour; crying as he opened the door, "Here is Mr. Grig, the favourite of the planets!"

'I will not attempt a description of female beauty, gentlemen, for every one of us has a model of his own that suits his own taste best. In this parlour that I'm speaking of, there were two young ladies; and if every gentleman present, will imagine two models of his own in their places, and will be kind enough to polish 'em up to the very highest pitch of perfection, he will then have a faint conception of their uncommon radiance.

'Besides these two young ladies, there was their waiting-woman, that under any other circumstances Tom would have looked upon as a Venus; and besides her, there was a tall, thin, dismal-faced young gentleman, half man and half boy, dressed in a childish suit of clothes very much too short in the legs and arms; and looking, according to Tom's comparison, like one of the wax juveniles from a tailor's door, grown up and run to seed. Now, this youngster stamped his foot upon the ground and looked very fierce at Tom, and Tom looked fierce at him - for to tell the truth, gentlemen, Tom more than half suspected that when they entered the room he was kissing one of the young ladies; and for anything Tom knew, you observe, it might be HIS young lady - which was not pleasant.

'"Sir," says Tom, "before we proceed any further, will you have the goodness to inform me who this young Salamander" - Tom called him that for aggravation, you perceive, gentlemen - "who this young Salamander may be?"

'"That, Mr. Grig," says the old gentleman, "is my little boy. He was christened Galile Isaac Newton Flamstead. Don't mind him. He's a mere child."

'"And a very fine child too," says Tom - still aggravating, you'll observe - "of his age and as good as fine, I have no doubt. How do you do, my man?" with which kind and patronising expressions, Tom reached up to pat him on the head, and quoted two lines about little boys, from Doctor Watts's Hymns, which he had learnt at a Sunday School.

'It was very easy to see, gentlemen, by this youngster's frowning and by the waiting-maid's tossing her head and turning up her nose, and by the young ladies turning their backs and talking together at the other end of the room, that nobody but the old gentleman took very kindly to the noble stranger. Indeed, Tom plainly heard the waiting-woman say of her master, that so far from being able to read the stars as he pretended, she didn't believe he knew his letters in 'em, or at best that

e had got further than words in one syllable; but Tom, not minding this (for he was
n spirits after the Madeira), looks with an agreeable air towards the young ladies,
nd, kissing his hand to both, says to the old gentleman, "Which is which?"

This," says the old gentleman, leading out the handsomest, if one of 'em could
ossibly be said to be handsomer than the other - "this is my niece, Miss Fanny
arker."

If you'll permit me, Miss," says Tom, "being a noble stranger and a favourite of the
lanets, I will conduct myself as such." With these words, he kisses the young lady
n a very affable way, turns to the old gentleman, slaps him on the back, and says,
When's it to come off, my buck?"

he young lady coloured so deep, and her lip trembled so much, gentlemen, that
om really thought she was going to cry. But she kept her feelings down, and
rning to the old gentleman, says, "Dear uncle, though you have the absolute
sposal of my hand and fortune, and though you mean well in disposing of 'em
us, I ask you whether you don't think this is a mistake? Don't you think, dear
ncle," she says, "that the stars must be in error? Is it not possible that the comet
ay have put 'em out?"

The stars," says the old gentleman, "couldn't make a mistake if they tried. Emma,"
e says to the other young lady.

Yes, papa," says she.

The same day that makes your cousin Mrs. Grig will unite you to the gifted
ooney. No remonstrance - no tears. Now, Mr. Grig, let me conduct you to that
allowed ground, that philosophical retreat, where my friend and partner, the gifted
ooney of whom I have just now spoken, is even now pursuing those discoveries
hich shall enrich us with the precious metal, and make us masters of the world.
ome, Mr. Grig," he says.

With all my heart, Sir," replies Tom; "and luck to the gifted Mooney, say I - not so
uch on his account as for our worthy selves!" With this sentiment, Tom kissed his
nd to the ladies again, and followed him out; having the gratification to perceive,
 he looked back, that they were all hanging on by the arms and legs of Galileo
aac Newton Flamstead, to prevent him from following the noble stranger, and
aring him to pieces.

entlemen, Tom's father-in-law that was to be, took him by the hand, and having
hted a little lamp, led him across a paved court-yard at the back of the house, into
very large, dark, gloomy room: filled with all manner of bottles, globes, books,
escopes, crocodiles, alligators, and other scientific instruments of every kind. In
e centre of this room was a stove or furnace, with what Tom called a pot, but
ich in my opinion was a crucible, in full boil. In one corner was a sort of ladder
ding through the roof; and up this ladder the old gentleman pointed, as he said in
whisper:

he observatory. Mr. Mooney is even now watching for the precise time at which
 are to come into all the riches of the earth. It will be necessary for he and I,

alone in that silent place, to cast your nativity before the hour arrives. Put the day and minute of your birth on this piece of paper, and leave the rest to me."

'"You don't mean to say," says Tom, doing as he was told and giving him back the paper, "that I'm to wait here long, do you? It's a precious dismal place."

'"Hush!" says the old gentleman. "It's hallowed ground. Farewell!"

'"Stop a minute," says Tom. "What a hurry you're in! What's in that large bottle yonder?"

'"It's a child with three heads," says the old gentleman; "and everything else in proportion."

'"Why don't you throw him away?" says Tom. "What do you keep such unpleasant things here for?"

'"Throw him away!" cries the old gentleman. "We use him constantly in astrology. He's a charm."

'"I shouldn't have thought it," says Tom, "from his appearance. MUST you go, I say?"

'The old gentleman makes him no answer, but climbs up the ladder in a greater bustle than ever. Tom looked after his legs till there was nothing of him left, and then sat down to wait; feeling (so he used to say) as comfortable as if he was going to be made a freemason, and they were heating the pokers.

'Tom waited so long, gentlemen, that he began to think it must be getting on for midnight at least, and felt more dismal and lonely than ever he had done in all his life. He tried every means of whiling away the time, but it never had seemed to move so slow. First, he took a nearer view of the child with three heads, and thought what a comfort it must have been to his parents. Then he looked up a long telescope which was pointed out of the window, but saw nothing particular, in consequence of the stopper being on at the other end. Then he came to a skeleton in a glass case, labelled, "Skeleton of a Gentleman - prepared by Mr. Mooney," - which made him hope that Mr. Mooney might not be in the habit of preparing gentlemen that way without their own consent. A hundred times, at least, he looked into the pot where they were boiling the philosopher's stone down to the proper consistency, and wondered whether it was nearly done. "When it is," thinks Tom, "I'll send out for six-penn'orth of sprats, and turn 'em into gold fish for a first experiment." Besides which, he made up his mind, gentlemen, to have a country-house and a park; and to plant a bit of it with a double row of gas-lamps a mile long, and go out every night with a French-polished mahogany ladder, and two servants in livery behind him, to light 'em for his own pleasure.

'At length and at last, the old gentleman's legs appeared upon the steps leading through the roof, and he came slowly down: bringing along with him, the gifted Mooney. This Mooney, gentlemen, was even more scientific in appearance than his friend; and had, as Tom often declared upon his word and honour, the dirtiest face we can possibly know of, in this imperfect state of existence.

"Gentlemen, you are all aware that if a scientific man isn't absent in his mind, he's of no good at all. Mr. Mooney was so absent, that when the old gentleman said to him, Shake hands with Mr. Grig," he put out his leg. "Here's a mind, Mr. Grig!" cries the old gentleman in a rapture. "Here's philosophy! Here's rumination! Don't disturb him," he says, "for this is amazing!"

Tom had no wish to disturb him, having nothing particular to say; but he was so uncommonly amazing, that the old gentleman got impatient, and determined to give him an electric shock to bring him to - "for you must know, Mr. Grig," he says, "that we always keep a strongly charged battery, ready for that purpose." These means being resorted to, gentlemen, the gifted Mooney revived with a loud roar, and he no sooner came to himself than both he and the old gentleman looked at Tom with compassion, and shed tears abundantly.

"My dear friend," says the old gentleman to the Gifted, "prepare him."

"I say," cries Tom, falling back, "none of that, you know. No preparing by Mr. Mooney if you please."

"Alas!" replies the old gentleman, "you don't understand us. My friend, inform him of his fate. - I can't."

The Gifted mustered up his voice, after many efforts, and informed Tom that his nativity had been carefully cast, and he would expire at exactly thirty-five minutes, twenty-seven seconds, and five- sixths of a second past nine o'clock, a.m., on that day two months.

Gentlemen, I leave you to judge what were Tom's feelings at this announcement, on the eve of matrimony and endless riches. "I think," he says in a trembling voice, "there must be a mistake in the working of that sum. Will you do me the favour to cast it up again?" - "There is no mistake," replies the old gentleman, "it is confirmed by Francis Moore, Physician. Here is the prediction for to-morrow two months." And he showed him the page, where sure enough were these words - "The decease of a great person may be looked for, about this time."

"Which," says the old gentleman, "is clearly you, Mr. Grig."

"Too clearly," cries Tom, sinking into a chair, and giving one hand to the old gentleman, and one to the Gifted. "The orb of day has set on Thomas Grig for ever!"

At this affecting remark, the Gifted shed tears again, and the other two mingled their tears with his, in a kind - if I may use the expression - of Mooney and Co.'s attire. But the old gentleman recovering first, observed that this was only a reason for hastening the marriage, in order that Tom's distinguished race might be transmitted to posterity; and requesting the Gifted to console Mr. Grig during his temporary absence, he withdrew to settle the preliminaries with his niece immediately.

And now, gentlemen, a very extraordinary and remarkable occurrence took place; for as Tom sat in a melancholy way in one chair, and the Gifted sat in a melancholy way in another, a couple of doors were thrown violently open, the two young ladies rushed in, and one knelt down in a loving attitude at Tom's feet, and the other at the Gifted's. So far, perhaps, as Tom was concerned - as he used to say - you will say there was nothing strange in this: but you will be of a different opinion when you understand that Tom's young lady was kneeling to the Gifted, and the Gifted's young lady was kneeling to Tom.

"'Halloa! stop a minute!" cries Tom; "here's a mistake. I need condoling with by sympathising woman, under my afflicting circumstances; but we're out in the figure. Change partners, Mooney."

"'Monster!" cries Tom's young lady, clinging to the Gifted.

"'Miss!" says Tom. "Is THAT your manners?"

"'I abjure thee!" cries Tom's young lady. "I renounce thee. I never will be thine. Thou," she says to the Gifted, "art the object of my first and all-engrossing passion. Wrapt in thy sublime visions, thou hast not perceived my love; but, driven to despair, I now shake off the woman and avow it. Oh, cruel, cruel man!" With which reproach she laid her head upon the Gifted's breast, and put her arms about him in the tenderest manner possible, gentlemen.

"'And I," says the other young lady, in a sort of ecstasy, that made Tom start - "I hereby abjure my chosen husband too. Hear me, Goblin!" - this was to the Gifted - "Hear me! I hold thee in the deepest detestation. The maddening interview of this one night has filled my soul with love - but not for thee. It is for thee, for thee, young man," she cries to Tom. "As Monk Lewis finely observes, Thomas, Thomas, I am thine, Thomas, Thomas, thou art mine: thine for ever, mine for ever!" with which words, she became very tender likewise.

'Tom and the Gifted, gentlemen, as you may believe, looked at each other in a very awkward manner, and with thoughts not at all complimentary to the two young ladies. As to the Gifted, I have heard Tom say often, that he was certain he was in fit, and had it inwardly.

"'Speak to me! Oh, speak to me!" cries Tom's young lady to the Gifted.

"'I don't want to speak to anybody," he says, finding his voice at last, and trying to push her away. "I think I had better go. I'm - I'm frightened," he says, looking about as if he had lost something.

"'Not one look of love!" she cries. "Hear me while I declare - "

"'I don't know how to look a look of love," he says, all in a maze. "Don't declare anything. I don't want to hear anybody."

"'That's right!" cries the old gentleman (who it seems had been listening). "That's right! Don't hear her. Emma shall marry you to-morrow, my friend, whether she likes it or not, and SHE shall marry Mr. Grig."

'Gentlemen, these words were no sooner out of his mouth than Galileo Isaac Newton Flamstead (who it seems had been listening too) darts in, and spinning round and round, like a young giant's top, cries, "Let her. Let her. I'm fierce; I'm furious. I give her leave. I'll never marry anybody after this - never. It isn't safe. She is the falsest of the false," he cries, tearing his hair and gnashing his teeth; "and I'll live and die a bachelor!"

"The little boy," observed the Gifted gravely, "albeit of tender years, has spoken wisdom. I have been led to the contemplation of woman-kind, and will not adventure on the troubled waters of matrimony."

"What!" says the old gentleman, "not marry my daughter! Won't you, Mooney? Not if I make her? Won't you? Won't you?"

"No," says Mooney, "I won't. And if anybody asks me any more, I'll run away, and never come back again."

"Mr. Grig," says the old gentleman, "the stars must be obeyed. You have not changed your mind because of a little girlish folly - eh, Mr. Grig?"

Tom, gentlemen, had had his eyes about him, and was pretty sure that all this was a device and trick of the waiting-maid, to put him off his inclination. He had seen her hiding and skipping about the two doors, and had observed that a very little whispering from her pacified the Salamander directly. "So," thinks Tom, "this is a plot - but it won't fit."

"Eh, Mr. Grig?" says the old gentleman.

Why, Sir," says Tom, pointing to the crucible, "if the soup's nearly ready - "

"Another hour beholds the consummation of our labours," returned the old gentleman.

Very good," says Tom, with a mournful air. "It's only for two months, but I may as well be the richest man in the world even for that time. I'm not particular, I'll take her, Sir. I'll take her."

The old gentleman was in a rapture to find Tom still in the same mind, and drawing the young lady towards him by little and little, was joining their hands by main force, when all of a sudden, gentlemen, the crucible blows up, with a great crash; everybody screams; the room is filled with smoke; and Tom, not knowing what may happen next, throws himself into a Fancy attitude, and says, "Come on, if you're a man!" without addressing himself to anybody in particular.

The labours of fifteen years!" says the old gentleman, clasping his hands and looking down upon the Gifted, who was saving the pieces, "are destroyed in an instant!" - And I am told, gentlemen, by-the-bye, that this same philosopher's stone would have been discovered a hundred times at least, to speak within bounds, if it hadn't for the one unfortunate circumstance that the apparatus always blows up, when it's on the very point of succeeding.

Tom turns pale when he hears the old gentleman expressing himself to this unpleasant effect, and stammers out that if it's quite agreeable to all parties, he would like to know exactly what has happened, and what change has really taken place in the prospects of that company.

'"We have failed for the present, Mr. Grig," says the old gentleman, wiping his forehead. "And I regret it the more, because I have in fact invested my niece's five thousand pounds in this glorious speculation. But don't be cast down," he says, anxiously - "in another fifteen years, Mr. Grig - "

"Oh!" cries Tom, letting the young lady's hand fall. "Were the stars very positive about this union, Sir?"

'"They were," says the old gentleman.

'"I'm sorry to hear it," Tom makes answer, "for it's no go, Sir."

'"No what!" cries the old gentleman.

'"Go, Sir," says Tom, fiercely. "I forbid the banns." And with these words - which are the very words he used - he sat himself down in a chair, and, laying his head upon the table, thought with a secret grief of what was to come to pass on that day two months.

'Tom always said, gentlemen, that that waiting-maid was the artfullest minx he had ever seen; and he left it in writing in this country when he went to colonize abroad, that he was certain in his own mind she and the Salamander had blown up the philosopher's stone on purpose, and to cut him out of his property. I believe Tom was in the right, gentlemen; but whether or no, she comes forward at this point, and says, "May I speak, Sir?" and the old gentleman answering, "Yes, you may," she goes on to say that "the stars are no doubt quite right in every respect, but Tom is not the man." And she says, "Don't you remember, Sir, that when the clock struck five this afternoon, you gave Master Galileo a rap on the head with your telescope, and told him to get out of the way?" "Yes, I do," says the old gentleman. "Then," says the waiting- maid, "I say he's the man, and the prophecy is fulfilled." The old gentleman staggers at this, as if somebody had hit him a blow on the chest, and cries, "He! why he's a boy!" Upon that, gentlemen, the Salamander cries out that he'll be twenty-one next Lady-day; and complains that his father has always been so busy with the sun round which the earth revolves, that he has never taken any notice of the son that revolves round him; and that he hasn't had a new suit of clothes since he was fourteen; and that he wasn't even taken out of nankeen frocks and trousers till he was quite unpleasant in 'em; and touches on a good many more family matters to the same purpose. To make short of a long story, gentlemen, the all talk together, and cry together, and remind the old gentleman that as to the noble family, his own grandfather would have been lord mayor if he hadn't died at a dinner the year before; and they show him by all kinds of arguments that if the cousins are married, the prediction comes true every way. At last, the old gentleman being quite convinced, gives in; and joins their hands; and leaves his daughter to marry anybody she likes; and they are all well pleased; and the Gifted as well as any of them.

'In the middle of this little family party, gentlemen, sits Tom all the while, as miserable as you like. But, when everything else is arranged, the old gentleman's aughter says, that their strange conduct was a little device of the waiting-maid's to disgust the lovers he had chosen for 'em, and will he forgive her? and if he will, perhaps he might even find her a husband - and when she says that, she looks uncommon hard at Tom. Then the waiting-maid says that, oh dear! she couldn't bear Mr. Grig should think she wanted him to marry her; and that she had even gone so far as to refuse the last lamplighter, who was now a literary character (having set up as a bill-sticker); and that she hoped Mr. Grig would not suppose she was on her last legs by any means, for the baker was very strong in his attentions at that moment, and as to the butcher, he was frantic. And I don't know how much more she might have said, gentlemen (for, as you know, this kind of young women are rare ones to talk), if the old gentleman hadn't cut in suddenly, and asked Tom if he'd have her, with ten pounds to recompense him for his loss of time and disappointment, and as a kind of bribe to keep the story secret.

It don't much matter, Sir," says Tom, "I ain't long for this world. Eight weeks of marriage, especially with this young woman, might reconcile me to my fate. I think," he says, "I could go off easy after that." With which he embraces her with a very dismal face, and groans in a way that might move a heart of stone - even of philosopher's stone.

Egad," says the old gentleman, "that reminds me - this bustle put it out of my head - there was a figure wrong. He'll live to a green old age - eighty-seven at least!"

How much, Sir?" cries Tom.

Eighty-seven!" says the old gentleman.

Without another word, Tom flings himself on the old gentleman's neck; throws up his hat; cuts a caper; defies the waiting-maid; and refers her to the butcher.

You won't marry her!" says the old gentleman, angrily.

And live after it!" says Tom. "I'd sooner marry a mermaid with a small-tooth comb and looking-glass."

Then take the consequences," says the other.

With those words - I beg your kind attention here, gentlemen, for it's worth your notice - the old gentleman wetted the forefinger of his right hand in some of the liquor from the crucible that was spilt on the floor, and drew a small triangle on Tom's forehead. The room swam before his eyes, and he found himself in the watch-house.'

Found himself WHERE?' cried the vice, on behalf of the company generally.

In the watch-house,' said the chairman. 'It was late at night, and he found himself in the very watch-house from which he had been let out that morning.'

Did he go home?' asked the vice.

'The watch-house people rather objected to that,' said the chairman; 'so he stopped there that night, and went before the magistrate in the morning. "Why, you're here again, are you?" says the magistrate, adding insult to injury; "we'll trouble you for five shillings more, if you can conveniently spare the money." Tom told him he had been enchanted, but it was of no use. He told the contractors the same, but they wouldn't believe him. It was very hard upon him, gentlemen, as he often said, for was it likely he'd go and invent such a tale? They shook their heads and told him he'd say anything but his prayers - as indeed he would; there's no doubt about that. It was the only imputation on his moral character that ever I heard of.'

## Our Bore

It is unnecessary to say that we keep a bore. Everybody does. But, the bore whom we have the pleasure and honour of enumerating among our particular friends, is such a generic bore, and has so many traits (as it appears to us) in common with the great bore family, that we are tempted to make him the subject of the present notes. May he be generally accepted!

Our bore is admitted on all hands to be a good-hearted man. He may put fifty people out of temper, but he keeps his own. He preserves a sickly solid smile upon his face, when other faces are ruffled by the perfection he has attained in his art, and has an equable voice which never travels out of one key or rises above one pitch. His manner is a manner of tranquil interest. None of his opinions are startling. Among his deepest-rooted convictions, it may be mentioned that he considers the air of England damp, and holds that our lively neighbours - he always calls the French our lively neighbours - have the advantage of us in that particular. Nevertheless he is unable to forget that John Bull is John Bull all the world over, and that England with all her faults is England still.

Our bore has travelled. He could not possibly be a complete bore without having travelled. He rarely speaks of his travels without introducing, sometimes on his own plan of construction, morsels of the language of the country - which he always translates. You cannot name to him any little remote town in France, Italy, Germany, or Switzerland but he knows it well; stayed there a fortnight under peculiar circumstances. And talking of that little place, perhaps you know a statue over an old fountain, up a little court, which is the second - no, the third - stay - yes, the third turning on the right, after you come out of the Post-house, going up the hill towards the market? You DON'T know that statue? Nor that fountain? You surprise him! They are not usually seen by travellers (most extraordinary, he has never yet met with a single traveller who knew them, except one German, the most intelligent man he ever met in his life!) but he thought that YOU would have been the man to find them out. And then he describes them, in a circumstantial lecture half an hour long, generally delivered behind a door which is constantly being opened from the other side; and implores you, if you ever revisit that place, now or go and look at that statue and fountain!

Our bore, in a similar manner, being in Italy, made a discovery of a dreadful picture, which has been the terror of a large portion of the civilized world ever since. We have seen the liveliest men paralysed by it, across a broad dining-table. He was ounging among the mountains, sir, basking in the mellow influences of the climate, when he came to UNA PICCOLA CHIESA - a little church - or perhaps it would be more correct to say UNA PICCOLISSIMA CAPPELLA - the smallest chapel you can possibly imagine - and walked in. There was nobody inside but a CIECO - a blind man - saying his prayers, and a VECCHIO PADRE - old friar-rattling a money-box. But, above the head of that friar, and immediately to the right of the altar as you enter - to the right of the altar? No. To the left of the altar as you enter - or say near the centre - there hung a painting (subject, Virgin and Child) so divine in its expression, so pure and yet so warm and rich in its tone, so fresh in its touch, at once so glowing in its colour and so statuesque in its repose, that our bore cried out in ecstasy, 'That's the finest picture in Italy!' And so it is, sir. There is no doubt of it. It is astonishing that that picture is so little known. Even the painter is uncertain. He afterwards took Blumb, of the Royal Academy (it is to be observed that our bore takes none but eminent people to see sights, and that none but eminent people take our bore), and you never saw a man so affected in your life as Blumb was. He cried like a child! And then our bore begins his description in detail - for all this is introductory - and strangles his hearers with the folds of the purple drapery.

By an equally fortunate conjunction of accidental circumstances, it happened that when our bore was in Switzerland, he discovered a Valley, of that superb character, that Chamouni is not to be mentioned in the same breath with it. This is how it was, sir. He was travelling on a mule - had been in the saddle some days - when, as he and the guide, Pierre Blanquo: whom you may know, perhaps? - our bore is sorry you don't, because he's the only guide deserving of the name - as he and Pierre were descending, towards evening, among those everlasting snows, to the little village of La Croix, our bore observed a mountain track turning off sharply to the right. At first he was uncertain whether it WAS a track at all, and in fact, he said to Pierre, 'QU'EST QUE C'EST DONC, MON AMI? - What is that, my friend? 'Ou, MONSIEUR!' said Pierre - 'Where, sir?' ' La! - there!' said our bore. 'MONSIEUR, CE N'EST RIEN DE TOUT - sir, it's nothing at all,' said Pierre. 'ALLONS! - Make haste. IL VA NEIGET - it's going to snow!' But, our bore was not to be done in that way, and he firmly replied, 'I wish to go in that direction - JE VEUX Y ALLER. I am bent upon it - JE SUIS DETERMINE. EN AVANT! - go ahead!' In consequence of which firmness on our bore's part, they proceeded, sir, during two hours of evening, and three of moonlight (they waited in a cavern till the moon was up), along the slenderest track, overhanging perpendicularly the most awful gulfs, until they arrived, by a winding descent, in a valley that possibly, and he may say probably, was never visited by any stranger before. What a valley! Mountains piled on mountains, avalanches hemmed by pine forests; waterfalls, chalets, mountain-torrents, wooden bridges, every conceivable picture of Swiss scenery! The whole village turned out to receive our bore. The peasant girls kissed him, the men shook hands with him, one old lady of benevolent appearance wept upon his breast. He was conducted, in a primitive triumph, to the little inn: where he was taken ill next morning, and lay for six weeks, attended by the amiable hostess (the same benevolent old lady who had wept over night) and her charming daughter, Fanchette. It is nothing to say that they were attentive to him; they doted on him. They called him in their simple way, L'ANGE ANGLAIS - the English Angel. When our bore left the valley, there was not a dry eye in the place; some of the people attended him for miles. He begs and entreats of you as a personal favour, that if you ever go to Switzerland again (you have mentioned that your last visit was your twenty-third), you will go to that valley, and see Swiss scenery for the first time. And if you want really to know the pastoral people of Switzerland, and to understand them, mention, in that valley, our bore's name!

Our bore has a crushing brother in the East, who, somehow or other, was admitted to smoke pipes with Mehemet Ali, and instantly became an authority on the whole range of Eastern matters, from Haroun Alraschid to the present Sultan. He is in the habit of expressing mysterious opinions on this wide range of subjects, but on questions of foreign policy more particularly, to our bore, in letters; and our bore is continually sending bits of these letters to the newspapers (which they never insert) and carrying other bits about in his pocket-book. It is even whispered that he has been seen at the Foreign Office, receiving great consideration from the messengers, and having his card promptly borne into the sanctuary of the temple. The havoc committed in society by this Eastern brother is beyond belief. Our bore is always ready with him. We have known our bore to fall upon an intelligent young sojourner in the wilderness, in the first sentence of a narrative, and beat all confidence out of him with one blow of his brother. He became omniscient, as to foreign policy, in the smoking of those pipes with Mehemet Ali. The balance of power in Europe, the machinations of the Jesuits, the gentle and humanising influence of Austria, the position and prospects of that hero of the noble soul who is worshipped by happy France, are all easy reading to our bore's brother. And our bore is so provokingly self-denying about him! 'I don't pretend to more than a very general knowledge of these subjects myself,' says he, after enervating the intellects of several strong men, 'but these are my brother's opinions, and I believe he is known to be well-informed.'

The commonest incidents and places would appear to have been made special, expressly for our bore. Ask him whether he ever chanced to walk, between seven and eight in the morning, down St. James's Street, London, and he will tell you, never in his life but once. But, it's curious that that once was in eighteen thirty; and that as our bore was walking down the street you have just mentioned, at the hour you have just mentioned - half-past seven - or twenty minutes to eight. No! Let him be correct! - exactly a quarter before eight by the palace clock - he met a fresh-coloured, grey- haired, good-humoured looking gentleman, with a brown umbrella, who, as he passed him, touched his hat and said, 'Fine morning, sir, fine morning!' William the Fourth!

Ask our bore whether he has seen Mr. Barry's new Houses of Parliament, and he will reply that he has not yet inspected them minutely, but, that you remind him that it was his singular fortune to be the last man to see the old Houses of Parliament before the fire broke out. It happened in this way. Poor John Spine, the celebrated novelist, had taken him over to South Lambeth to read to him the last few chapters of what was certainly his best book - as our bore told him at the time, adding, 'Now my dear John, touch it, and you'll spoil it!' - and our bore was going back to the club by way of Millbank and Parliament Street, when he stopped to think of Canning, and look at the Houses of Parliament. Now, you know far more of the philosophy of Mind than our bore does, and are much better able to explain to him than he is to explain to you why or wherefore, at that particular time, the thought of fire should come into his head. But, it did. It did. He thought, What a national calamity if an edifice connected with so many associations should be consumed by fire! At that time there was not a single soul in the street but himself. All was quiet, dark, and solitary. After contemplating the building for a minute - or, say a minute and a half, not more - o bore proceeded on his way, mechanically repeating, What a national calamity if such an edifice, connected with such associations, should be destroyed by - A man coming towards him in a violent state of agitation completed the sentence, with the exclamation, Fire! Our bore looked round, and the whole structure was in a blaze.

In harmony and union with these experiences, our bore never went anywhere in a steamboat but he made either the best or the worst voyage ever known on that station. Either he overheard the captain say to himself, with his hands clasped, 'We are all lost!' or the captain openly declared to him that he had never made such a run before, and never should be able to do it again. Our bore was in that express train on that railway, when they made (unknown to the passengers) the experiment of going at the rate of a hundred to miles an hour. Our bore remarked on that occasion to the other people in the carriage, 'This is too fast, but sit still!' He was at the Norwich musical festival when the extraordinary echo for which science has been wholly unable to account, was heard for the first and last time. He and the bishop heard it at the same moment, and caught each other's eye. He was present at that illumination of St. Peter's, of which the Pope is known to have remarked, as he looked at it out of his window in the Vatican, 'O CIELO! QUESTA COSA NON SARA FATTA, MAI ANCORA, COME QUESTA - O Heaven! this thing will never be done again, like this!' He has seen every lion he ever saw, under some remarkably propitious circumstances. He knows there is no fancy in it, because in every case the showman mentioned the fact at the time, and congratulated him upon it.

At one period of his life, our bore had an illness. It was an illness of a dangerous character for society at large. Innocently remark that you are very well, or that somebody else is very well; and our bore, with a preface that one never knows what a blessing health is until one has lost it, is reminded of that illness, and drags you through the whole of its symptoms, progress, and treatment. Innocently remark that you are not well, or that somebody else is not well, and the same inevitable result ensues. You will learn how our bore felt a tightness about here, sir, for which he couldn't account, accompanied with a constant sensation as if he were being stabbed - or, rather, jobbed - that expresses it more correctly - jobbed - with a blunt knife. Well, sir! This went on, until sparks began to flit before his eyes, water-wheels to turn round in his head, and hammers to beat incessantly, thump, thump, thump, all down his back - along the whole of the spinal vertebrae. Our bore, when his sensations had come to this, thought it a duty he owed to himself to take advice, and he said, Now, whom shall I consult? He naturally thought of Callow, at that time one of the most eminent physicians in London, and he went to Callow. Callow said, liver!' and prescribed rhubarb and calomel, low diet, and moderate exercise. Our bore went on with this treatment, getting worse every day, until he lost confidence in Callow, and went to Moon, whom half the town was then mad about. Moon was interested in the case; to do him justice he was very much interested in the case; and he said, 'Kidneys!' He altered the whole treatment, sir - gave strong acids, cupped, and blistered. This went on, our bore still getting worse every day, until he openly told Moon it would be a satisfaction to him if he would have a consultation with Clatter. The moment Clatter saw our bore, he said, 'Accumulation of fat about the heart!' Snugglewood, who was called in with him, differed, and said, 'Brain!' But, what they all agreed upon was, to lay our bore upon his back, to shave his head, to leech him, to administer enormous quantities of medicine, and to keep him low; so that he was reduced to a mere shadow, you wouldn't have known him, and nobody considered it possible that he could ever recover. This was his condition, sir, when he heard of Jilkins - at that period in a very small practice, and living in the upper part of a house in Great Portland Street; but still, you understand, with a rising reputation among the few people to whom he was known. Being in that condition in which a drowning man catches at a straw, our bore sent for Jilkins. Jilkins came. Our bore liked his eye, and said, 'Mr. Jilkins, I have a presentiment that you will do me good.' Jilkins's reply was characteristic of the man. It was, 'Sir, I mean to do you good.' This confirmed our bore's opinion of his eye, and they went into the case together - went completely into it. Jilkins then got up, walked across the room, came back, and sat down. His words were these. 'You have been humbugged. This is a case of indigestion, occasioned by deficiency of power in the Stomach. Take a mutton chop in half-an- hour, with a glass of the finest old sherry that can be got for money. Take two mutton chops to-morrow, and two glasses of the finest old sherry. Next day, I'll come again.' In a week our bore was on his legs, and Jilkins's success dates from that period!

Our bore is great in secret information. He happens to know many things that nobody else knows. He can generally tell you where the split is in the Ministry; he knows a great deal about the Queen; and has little anecdotes to relate of the royal nursery. He gives you the judge's private opinion of Sludge the murderer, and his thoughts when he tried him. He happens to know what such a man got by such a transaction, and it was fifteen thousand five hundred pounds, and his income is twelve thousand a year. Our bore is also great in mystery. He believes, with an exasperating appearance of profound meaning, that you saw Parkins last Sunday? - Yes, you did. - Did he say anything particular? - No, nothing particular. - Our bore is surprised at that. - Why? - Nothing. Only he understood that Parkins had come to tell you something. - What about? - Well! our bore is not at liberty to mention what about. But, he believes you will hear that from Parkins himself, soon, and he hopes it may not surprise you as it did him. Perhaps, however, you never heard about Parkins's wife's sister? - No. - Ah! says our bore, that explains it!

Our bore is also great in argument. He infinitely enjoys a long humdrum, drowsy interchange of words of dispute about nothing. He considers that it strengthens the mind, consequently, he 'don't see that,' very often. Or, he would be glad to know what you mean by that. Or, he doubts that. Or, he has always understood exactly the reverse of that. Or, he can't admit that. Or, he begs to deny that. Or, surely you don't mean that. And so on. He once advised us; offered us a piece of advice, after the fact, totally impracticable and wholly impossible of acceptance, because it supposed the fact, then eternally disposed of, to be yet in abeyance. It was a dozen years ago, and to this hour our bore benevolently wishes, in a mild voice, on certain regular occasions, that we had thought better of his opinion.

The instinct with which our bore finds out another bore, and closes with him, is amazing. We have seen him pick his man out of fifty men, in a couple of minutes. They love to go (which they do naturally) into a slow argument on a previously exhausted subject, and to contradict each other, and to wear the hearers out, without impairing their own perennial freshness as bores. It improves the good understanding between them, and they get together afterwards, and bore each other amicably. Whenever we see our bore behind a door with another bore, we know that when he comes forth, he will praise the other bore as one of the most intelligent men he ever met. And this bringing us to the close of what we had to say about our bore, we are anxious to have it understood that he never bestowed this raise on us.

## Charles Dickens - A Short Biography

Charles Dickens (1812-1870) is regarded by many readers and literary critics to be THE major English novelist of the Victorian Age. He is remembered today as the author of a series of weighty novels which have been translated into many languages and promoted to the rank of World Classics. The latter include, but are not limited to, *The Adventures of Oliver Twist*, *A Tale of Two Cities*, *David Copperfield*, *A Christmas Carol*, *Hard Times*, *Great Expectations* and *The Old Curiosity Shop*.

## Birth and Childhood's Hardships

By and large, Charles Dickens's life story is one of somebody who is born and raised in dire straits to become one of the greatest men who have marked human history and thought. It is a perfect example of how the plight of the deprived and the destitute could transform into a precious incentive that pushes them to challenge their circumstances and to unexpectedly excel and shine.

Charles Dickens was born in Portsmouth on February 7$^{th}$, 1812. His father John Dickens worked as a simple accounting clerk at the Naval Pay Office and the family's pecuniary situation was almost always uneven. When Charles was only two years, the family had to move to London, then later to Chatham. For financial reasons, Charles did not have adequate education. He rather had to leave school at a very young age to work at a polishing and blacking factory. To add insult to injury, Charles's father was imprisoned in 1824 after failing to pay a 40-pound debt.

Charles's experience at the factory played a tremendous role in building the novelist's personality and in deepening his concerns about working children and about the working class in general. Dickens's precocious maturity and the serious responsibilities that he had as a little child left a clear impression on many of his young characters, such as Oliver Twist, David Copperfield and Pip in *Great Expectations*. The hardships that Charles Dickens personally went through made him much interested in defending the poor, in fighting social injustice through exposing its blatant manifestations and in accentuating the importance of having decent work conditions.

Between 1824 and 1827, Dickens's father, who eventually managed to pay his debts, offered Charles the opportunity to attend a private school in North London, the Wellington House Academy. The experience surely enriched the young man's knowledge of the rules of writing and rhetoric and whetted his appetite for 18<sup>th</sup>-century novels and for the picaresque novels that adorned his father's library. However, during this period, Charles still had to experience another disappointment when his mother refused to spare him the strenuous job at the blacking factory even after the relative improvement of the family's financial situation. The mother's decision had a great psychological impact on young Charles and even influenced his vision of gender roles as he thought that the mother should not be the decision-maker in the family.

**Early Publications**

Young Charles Dickens occupied numerous jobs and worked hard to learn shorthand. This long and diversified professional experience had a patent impact on his different writings. Indeed, after the blacking factory experience, Dickens first worked as a clerk for attorneys, which allowed him to learn about the legal system and its principles, to become a free-lance reporter for Doctor's Commons Courts in 1829. Later, he even wrote reports for the House of Commons before starting to work for newspapers, magazines and journals.

It was in 1833 that Dickens started writing short stories for a number of literary magazines and journals such as *The Monthly Magazine*. A collection of these texts was later pseudonymously published under the title *Sketches by Boz*. Thanks to Dickens's humor and exceptional writing style, the latter publication was relatively successful, but not as successful as *The Pickwick Papers* whose serial publication sold thousands of copies and raised Dickens to considerable fame. In 1836, he started writing short texts to be published with the humorous illustrations of the famous artist Robert Seymour. These first successes encouraged Dickens to carry on publishing other stories in the form of series. Dickens's next creation was *Oliver Twist* which was published between 1837 and 1839.

It is noteworthy that most of Dickens's novels were published in the form of monthly and weekly chapters which, according to critics and biographers, allowed him to evaluate and adjust his characterizations and plots to meet the expectations of his readership. It was also during this period that Dickens started his long career as a literary magazine editor.

**Loves and Marriage**

Charles Dickens got married on April 2<sup>nd</sup>, 1836 to Catherine Thomson Hogarth after one year of engagement. They settled at the famous urnival's Inn in Holborn, London, before they moved to their home in Bloomsbury. The house was transformed into the Charles Dickens Museum in 1925. Charles and Catherine, who lived there with the first three of their ten children, were joined by Charles's brother Frederick and Catherine's sister Mary. The latter was reported to have had a very special place in Charles's heart. After dying in his own arms in 1837 following a sudden illness, she became a source of inspiration for some of his female characters. After three years of marriage, Dickens's success and rising income made him leave the house for larger and more luxurious estates.

Catherine Hogarth was not Dickens's only love, however. Indeed, biographers report that Dickens's relation with his wife was sandwiched by two other romantic affairs. First, there was Maria Beadnell, a banker's daughter, with whom Dickens fell in love when he was only eighteen years old. The relationship ended three years later when Maria's parents apparently intervened. The other love story that Dickens went through started in 1857 and pushed him to divorce Catherine the following year. It was when Dickens was having a group of young actresses for the staging of his play *The Frozen Deep* that he fell in love with the actress Ellen Ternan who was 27 years younger than him.


## Major Achievements

Charles's first success with *The Pickwick Papers* and *Oliver Twist* only pushed him to devote more time and energy to his writing and editorial activities. After publishing *Nicholas Nickleby* between 1838 and 1839, he started a new project in 1840 that he entitled *Master Humphrey's Clock*. The latter is a collection of stories that share the same frame and have recurring characters. It was among this collection that the two major works *The Old Curiosity Shop* and *Barnaby Rudge* were serially published.

After visiting the United States of America in 1842, Dickens developed a rather negative view of the New World which was mainly depicted in his travelogue *American Notes for General Circulation* and also in his picaresque novel *Martin Chuzzlewit*. The latter included very harsh satire of the republic and strongly denounced its institution of slavery. However, the fury that Dickens caused among some American circles was soon quietened with the publication of *A Christmas Carol* in 1843. The book, which is considered by many as the novelist's finest opus, was celebrated both in England and America.

Two other Christmas books followed respectively in 1834 and 1845. They are *The Chimes* and *The Cricket on the Hearth*. During this period, Dickens also published a new travelogue that he entitled *Pictures from Italy* following his stay in the Mediterranean country. Another Christmas story entitled *The Haunted Man* was published in 1848, which was preceded by *Dombey and Son* (1847) and *The Battle of Life* (1847) and followed by David Copperfield (1849-1850), *Bleak House* (1852-1853) and *Hard Times* (1854).

It was in 1853 that Dickens started organizing public performances in which he presented his literary works. By this time, he also started to collaborate with Wilkie Collins on a number of short stories and plays. *Little Dorrit* started as a monthly serial in 1855 to be finished in 1857. Later, two of Dickens's most valuable works were published: *A Tale of Two Cities* (1859) and *Great Expectations* (1861). They were both published in the weekly periodical, *All the Year Round*, which he founded and edited himself.

Apart from his writings, Dickens's main profitable activity was the public reading of his novels. Along with the money he earned thanks to his successful publications, public readings allowed Dickens to buy his dream house (Gad's Hill Place, Kent),  to offer financial help to his parents and brothers and to engage in charitable activities.


**Twilight and Death**

During the 1860s, Dickens carried on organizing more reading tours. In addition to the many events he had in England, he visited France, the United States, Scotland and Ireland on many an occasion. In 1864, he started his last complete novel, *Our Mutual Friend*. However, by 1865, his health started to waver. This was mainly because of the physical and intellectual exhaustion to which he subjected himself. Furthermore, Dickens was psychologically traumatized in 1865 following a train crash. He was with his beloved Ellen Ternan on their way back from Paris when their train derailed to cause a big number of casualties. Although Dickens was able to collect his courage and managed to help the wounded and comfort them, the picture of the disaster affected him greatly and could never be erased from his mind.

For health reasons, Dickens cancelled many of his programmed readings between 1868 and 1870. On April 22nd, 1869, he had a stroke. The latter was followed by a second stroke on June 8th, 1870, while he was working on his novel *The Mystery of Edwin Drood* which would remain unfinished. The next day, he passed away. Charles Dickens today rests in The Poets' Corner of Westminster Abbey.

www.ingramcontent.com/pod-product-compliance
Lightning Source LLC
Chambersburg PA
CBHW061456170626
46811CB00004B/1531